The Park Bench

The Park Bench

HENRY VON DOUSSA

Clouds of Magellan Press | Melbourne

This edition published 2021 by Clouds of Magellan Press. Melbourne, Australia

ISBN: 978-0-6453531-0-5 (hardback)

ISBN: 978-0-6453531-1-2 (paperback)

Originally published in 2006 by Arcadia, an imprint of Australian Scholarly Publishing

www.cloudsofmagellanpress.net

Foreword

Engaging again with the *The Park Bench* in preparation for a new edition I was struck enormously by the isolation and hope for connection of Lenny the protagonist. The marginalisation he experiences as a gay man is brutal, thorough, unrelenting. The sense that his gayness is unbecoming—his sexual needs a deficit—he both internalises and projects onto the men he meets, who, for the most part, he despises and needs in equal parts. Fifteen years after first publication, I was also struck by the mechanism Lenny uses in the midst of anguish and agitation to release emotional pressure and to find rest. For Lenny, anonymous, brief sexual connections are the release valve; and the park bench, which he describes as a faithful old friend, is the place he has found to quietly sit and rest when a lonely, dingy flat, surrounded by the intrusion of other people's lives, is the last place to which he wants to return. Lenny is a tough character, a hardy man in his late 20s grieving the loss of a relationship and figuring out how to rebuild and find self-worth. The public toilet, designed to drain away society's filth, is a place he hopes might drain away the failure, the bleakness, the anger—the filth he feels inside. It is also a place—along with the surrounding parks—where he goes to connect with other outsiders.

In the article, 'Privacy could only be had in public: Gay uses of the street', George Chauncy writes, 'There is no queer space, there are only spaces used by queers or put to queer use.' Chauncy charts the history of queer outsiders struggling to find spaces to connect with other gay men when the legal and social constraints of the day preclude them from living as they like and moving freely—safely—through both private space (the home) and public space.

> The city streets and parks served as vital meeting grounds for men who lived with their families or in cramped quarters with few amenities, and the vitality and diversity of the gay street scene attracted many other men as well. Streets and parks were where many men—'queer' and 'normal' alike—went to find sexual partners, where many men went to socialize, and where many men went for sex and ended up being socialized into the gay world.[1]

The men scattered through *The Park Bench* are emblematic of the men and the experiences Chauncy describes, and show why, even now in the face of society's relative openness to LGBTIQ+ lives and spaces, a commercial gay nightclub or commercial sex venue might still, because of fear and unknowing, be less available than less queer spaces put to queer use. Tony, an older heterosexual married father from the book, sees men cruising in a park when he goes jogging and entertains for the first time since he'd had gay sex as an adolescent, the possibility of enacting desires that have silently stewed in him for forty years. Tony would not have gone to a commercial gay venue.

At the time of writing the book (2003-2005) I was heavily influenced, as I am today, by the writings of the French historian Michelle Foucault, and by Foucault's project: to explore and address the relationship between

---

[1] Elia, M. M. (1996). *Stud: Architectures of masculinity* (Vol. 3). Princeton Architectural Press.

power and knowledge, and how they are used as a form of social control through societal institutions such as the school, the church, the prison system, medicine, psychiatry. Foucault was interested in how the human self is produced by the systems in which it sits, what we can and can't do—what we are forced to become—through discourse. But, Foucault says, 'Where there is power, there is resistance'. I hope in *The Park Bench* to have rendered the constraints and the traps life throws up, and, most importantly, the quick-release mechanisms that are used when constraint becomes intolerable.

Since 2005 there have been a few significant legal and policy changes to improve LGBTIQ+ lives. Of course, mostly widely publicised was the passing of the same-sex marriage equality bill in 2017. Having the country vote on whether same-sex attracted people should have the right to affirm their love through marriage—and all the discussion it generated—was very hurtful and damaged many family relationships. In 2008 changes in Victoria to the *Assisted Reproductive Treatment Act* made way for improved possibilities and access for lesbian women and gay men to create families and have children with relative legal security (the laws surrounding IVF and surrogacy, same-sex couples and parental responsibility remain complex and uneven across different Australian jurisdictions); for the first time two mothers (but not two fathers) could have their names on a child's birth certificate. In 2014 (and later in other Australian jurisdictions) the Australian Capital Territory abolished the sex reassignment surgery requirement for a change of sex marker on birth certificates, in so doing abolishing many constraints to trans and gender diverse people obtaining legal documents consistent with their affirmed gender. As a result of this reform, people are now free to self-nominate their sex as male, female or many other non-binary descriptors of their choice. The last decade has seen many changes in Australia related to laws around gender affirmation.

In 2021, *The Change or Suppression (Conversion) Practices Prohibition* Bill was passed in Victoria to make it illegal for religious institutions, schools, counsellors, psychiatry etc. to try to change or suppress a person's sexual orientation or gender identity. Much psychological damage and many suicides have been the result of these past practices for people trying to affirm their sexuality or gender. Additionally, it was only in 2016 that the many Victorian men who until 1981 were charged with homosexual offences and faced penalties of up to 15 years' jail had their criminal records expunged. Until then, they lived, and many died, as criminals.

Regardless of these important changes, LGBTIQ+ people still experience discrimination and marginalisation, and fare significantly poorer on many mental health measures when compared with the general population. LGBTIQ+ youth in regional or remotes area of Australia (like the character of Bruce set in the town of Nhill) are seven times more likely to end their own lives than heterosexual cisgender youth. In this regard, while rereading this work seemed to me sad—brutal even—it is not passé or redundant. My hope is, if *The Park Bench* is rereleased again in fifteen years' time, that it will feel old hat.

Henry von Doussa, November 2021

Here we go again

The end started at a dance party in the Hi-Fi Club on Swanston Street. Such pretty, lolly-like colours in the plastic bag, one hardly seemed enough in the hand and then in the mouth. Pills like the softest powder-pink drops from a Pez dispenser, but rancid-strong, which we'd stopped expecting, were unprepared for.

'At the very least ...' he said.

I hummed and ha'd, then went along, swallowing one, then, with impatience, another about fifteen minutes later.

After the fight in the taxi and more missing money, I'd been apprehensive about the whole evening.

'At the very least, let's just chuck a few back and dance.'

We danced together on a podium above the crowd. Nothing special, just the two of us on top of the world. Fantastic. People looked up at us and we looked down on them, and somehow it all felt in place, as it should be, just so.

Boys with arms in the air. Hundreds of sweaty arms. Some with cigarettes, some with bottles of water. Some playing with the laser lights in a sea of bodies, twirling fingers through the splatterings of lime green, some with eyes closed and one hundred percent oblivious.

Stolly Philosopher On Life blowing hard at the whistle on a fluoro string round his neck. For once not dribbling shit about how he saw the world, not giving New Age advice that you never asked for—but which he made yours anyway. Dancing and blowing the whistle to his own internal rhythms we guessed because he was out of time as hell with the music.

Peeking smiles and white teeth flashed up from the dance floor. Usually looked and looked away quick. I pointed my finger like a gun at a pair of pumped biceps in studded leather bands. Pointed and smiled and cracked a pose to scrunch the muscles around my abs. Cracked the same pose over and over to get an audience. Sometimes hitting my fists against my tough gut in time to the music. Sometimes running my fist over taut muscles to make them a washboard. Shit-hot and loving it. Cracked poses with hands behind my head like Arnie might do, so my body was shaped like an S and the lower ab muscles on each side stood out like arrows shooting into my pants. Fingers matted in my sweaty blonde hair as I flexed, then all hair flung back with sweat spraying off the sun-kissed tips. Shit-hot and loving it.

When the pills took hold with full force *What it Feels Like for a Girl* was playing. Not yet a hit, but Madonna could do no wrong. And of course the song had us, really upping the ante as we toyed with layers of feigned masculinity. Arms cut through ballistic lasers flicking in time to the remix. Beaded sweat turned to tears down my face, then licked into my mouth. Chucking poses and firing clip after clip from double-barrelled fingers into the crowd.

Daniel started losing it right about then. Down from the podium, through the crowd quickly as you can, walking on warping floors with strobing eyes. The music, the people, the smells, his close proximity to me, the colour and the light, all rolled into one and threatened to bowl him over.

Been together for five years of love and trouble. Open relationship with rules. Rules broken. Closed relationship with rules. Affairs. Love and long patches of monogamy with cooked breakfasts and lazy mornings. Love and gonorrhoea, chlamydia, crabs in the bad times. Rented flats, rented houses, sometimes sharing with friends to save money. Same bed, separate beds, same money, separate money. Money gone for the habit. Money just plain gone. Pawned VCR and telly. New ones for Christmas and sometimes gone by Easter.

Taking control, I bought a bottle of red water and we headed for the toilets. Sleazy Hi-Fi Club toilets. Post-AIDS education posters gaffer-taped to the cracked tiles. No messages on the posters, just downloaded photos, fisting, fucking, slings, tied-up trade, needles and piercings. A guy having his mouth pissed into above the urinal. No messages in post-AIDS education—Just Do It—and then condom and lube packs dumped in piles near sinks and on top of cisterns. Needle bins in cubicles. Do it safe or bareback it. Just Do It.

We sat in a cubicle, away from the crashing music that funnelled in, loud then soft, when the main door banged open. I smoked a Stuyvy, but Daniel was too far gone even for that. I held his hand. I stroked it and encouraged him to tell me what he was feeling. But I was chatty, wanting more than the grunts I got back.

Men not pissing, not doing anything but hanging around the urinal. A line for the other two cubicles didn't move. People wanting to take whatever they couldn't easily swallow with a swig on the dance floor or at the bar, wanting to scoff their wee trails of snow off the tip of the cistern, that would need a wipe down first.

Daniel sat on the closed toilet lid and I squatted against the partition, the paper dispenser level with my shoulder, but no paper. With the cubicle door open, some glared from the line, but we were in no hurry. Mostly leather and latex on the bodies but we went in with jeans, having gotten past The Beef on the door—who was there as much as anything to keep the dress code.

A leather queen with a six pack of flabs poked his head in, sucking in his gut when I looked up. But Daniel couldn't give a rats. I didn't give a shit either. Dimpled bum cheeks spilling out of polished chaps is what I saw as he turned and walked away.

For fifteen minutes or so (which felt like hours) I talked Daniel through the whole gorgeous catastrophe. I loved it. He needed me. I was sure of it.

'Top score, baby. My hands are tingling. I can't touch my fingers together. They're kickin' in now. You alright, Dan? It was a good decision to come, hey. I've missed you, babe … when we fight. I've missed going out. We're good for each other. We need each other, I know. Sorry about

4

the taxi. That driver … what an arsehole. He said some bloody thing when we got out. Jerk. We're good though, baby.'

His head was down. I kissed his hand. 'Sweetheart,' I said, 'just keep breathing, it's okay. The worst has already happened. The worst is over.'

He trembled and sweated in a way that told me he was committed and strong, a regular tough guy in for the long haul. Able to withstand what was chucked his way. Fragile now, crumbled, but strong as an ox. Durable. He sipped at the water. Looked at me. Eyes worried but sparkling. White Doves, Huggies, Pokemon, Super Novas, they had him. Even though he was able to show me where he'd come from and who he hoped to be—even on the dance floor with arms going spastic in the air—he was holding back, even after five years, still measuring his trust.

'Lennie,' he said back, 'sometimes I feel nothing.'

Sweat beaded on his forehead. He took long precise breaths, the kind you take when you're convincing yourself you can keep going a little longer, not passing out yet, with vomit curling like a question mark up the gut to the back of the throat. Breaths that you're living in because that's where every bit of your concentration goes to make them happen. Still, I wanted more, the big scene, melodrama, Something. I was flying.

'You're trembling,' I said, thinking of the dance floor. I half stood and pulled at his arm.

'Bit longer. Stay …' with dribble he said, looking down. Hands sweat, face sweat, t-shirt lost, hair still looking great. People milled around the toilet. 'Just get on with it!' To which I gave a phony grin, and relaxed. I loved it. He was with me. My man. There on the cubicle floor I held on. He stayed with me when in every other way he was gone. He held my hand and shook and went pale as a band-aid, but hung in. He showed me his mettle.

'This is it,' I kept telling myself. 'He's the one, my main event.'

And yet.

Me still deciding even after five years, still measuring how much I wanted him, even then. Me not giving in to him when he said I love you, still keeping one eye turned out to the side, scoping for a better option. Me going up Brunswick Street not a hundred percent his, rubber-necking like a bitch on heat, even when we were walking and I was holding his proud-as-you-like hand.

Not long after that ballistic night something changed. Maybe we'd gone too far to ever come back, and who the hell has the conviction to live that exposed, to live life like a raw nerve? We tried. For the next few weekends we partied. Hard. The highs, the dancing, the comedowns. We partied to keep from noticing we were all but done. We played it right out, squeezing out every last drop of faith or goodwill until, in the supermarket, I heard myself saying, 'Muesli, not Weetbix', with such meanness I hardly recognised myself. Under the neon lights at the Fifteen Items or Less I just stuck my head in the TV Week and said nothing. At the BP I made him do the pumping then yelled 'Run' out the wound-down window because the dawdle in his walk to pay was leaving me in ribbons. Still he didn't run and then we said nothing the whole way home in the car.

Soon enough Daniel stopped completely. He stopped showing me who he was and who he hoped to become. Soon just passed each other in the house and no longer made a date for *The Price Is Right* on the days he was on an early and home by five. No longer sat where we once held hands on the couch and yelled at the scrubbers who'd put the Versace watch before the barbecue in the showcase. No longer got to see his face light up from someone else's good luck. The froth and bubble gone and I'd cry about it if I still could.

Daniel turned away. He looked in the other direction, over the back fence and down the street. Way down High Street towards the city. Looked past what we'd tried to hold onto by our last move, which was, I think, move number four, almost one for each year of our lives together. Stuff in storage in the Flemington lock-up, stuff in a shed in Adelaide, and the clothes and club chairs in the Fitzroy lean-to. Lives in transit and spread too thin.

Once he turned, it was only a short way through the parks of Fairfield and North Fitzroy, across Alexandra Parade, back to the pubs and clubs of the inner city. It was only a short way from Preston to Collingwood. It didn't take long for Friday night to come around. And for me to reappear. I stood with a Stuyvy and a glass of beer, me leaning against the carpeted walls of a reliable club, perhaps in the groove I'd made years before as I waited for Dan to walk up and offer to buy me a drink. Perhaps in a furrow that foresaw my return and was waiting, kept warm by a man who, for the moment, was away taking a leak, buying another round, or, if he was lucky, following a dream and a hardening dick back to Doncaster or

Vermont South, away from the grey haze from cigarettes and the smoke machine. That's what the nightlife depended on, the booze, the drugs, the porn on the monitors behind the bar, cheap titillation that padded out the time spent trying to find each other. But for the most part, it was tough work, it lost its lustre fast, so once you'd found a man, once you'd paired up, you returned to the suburbs to rest, grateful to have what you'd been told for so long would be impossible. I had found a spot to stand and watch. To hope. But I was over it.

'Fuck you then, Len, I've had it,' Daniel yelled, face like a bull, but I was the one kicking up dust. After him down the steps and didn't give a rats about the neighbours. No. 7's probably got his snout at the fly-wire. There's a greasy stain from how he pushed in hard to get a better gander. He never goes out so why should I put drama on hold for privacy?

'Your moods. Your resentment. Your whingeing, God. So, I screwed up. I lost it for a bit. Lost my job. I lost myself for a while there, but you can't let it be. Just can't let it rest. I've been going under and instead of giving a shit you carry on like a fucking pork chop. I could be dying and all I get from you ...'

'You're already dead, you just don't know it yet,' I yelled towards the car space. He didn't turn or anything so I go, 'That's it? That's it?'

Then STUFF YOU to the back of the Adidas jacket.

The gravel's pretty sharp on my bare feet, even though most times I can butt a Stuyvy out on them. Stolly Philosopher On Life reckons it's a top party trick, and I suppose it is. Anyway, I wasn't running after something

I'd already been chasing for five years. Too tired. Been bruised and hurt enough already without adding feet to the list of damaged goods.

Him in the car. Wheels spinning and spitting gravel in a way that reminded me of fun back home: doughnuts, burn-outs, circle work in the old ute my uncle had on the farm. Dan's car twitched when it grabbed the bitumen, left a couple of Ss and was gone.

Daniel was gone.

No-one in the street. All working or shopping or having a life. Only the sun and No. 7 looked on and I couldn't care less about them. The other flats dormant, dead as, which was a relief. Sex and fights, the two things you never want to hear in a group of flats, the two things that made me cover my ears when it was someone else, but which I, in the middle of, couldn't keep to myself, wouldn't hold back. Sex and fights travelled between the thin brick walls, the threadbare carpets, the ceilings. When they happened, people sat up and noticed.

More than anything, more than the smell of someone else's cooking food or the loud gurgling of an old Holden being fired up and left to warm up under your window early on a cold morning, this is what I remembered about the strangers who lived around us; how a sudden burst of noise would make me uneasy, angry.

I sat down on the step and everything I could've done different was running through me. I lit a Stuyvy. The sun caught the smoke and made it thick and blue and extra heavy. Maybe all the shit they say is true. Between being

9

shaky and beside myself I knew I was wearing out fast, like my use-by date was looming and any moment soon I'd be marked down and shipped out. Brown tar on my fingers. Couldn't wash it off so it was there to stay. Dirt under my nails, even with some bitten back to the quick. Scars on my hands from stupid shit and rough stuff as a kid. My middle finger's just like Mum's, high on the right then down sharp to the finger next to the thumb. They smell of smoke like hers too.

Him-speeding-off's fingers smell the same, and it's hello yesterday, with his fingers in my face or down my throat, with me here and there and all over the place in the bed, thinking of the old girl when he's in me.

The sun on my back and me doing a Dorothy with my feet. I clicked my heels and on the count of three was still there. A half circle in the gravel made by my heels was like the start of a love heart or the wings of a bird flying. I dragged on the butt of a Stuyvy then ditched it in the grass.

Daniel was gone for good.

Failure

I felt cheated and a failure, a not-quite-right type of person who couldn't succeed in a world of slick images. A world we'd been sold; a world I couldn't replicate or repel. L'Oreo pro-styling range, Indola PE Complex, Schwarzkopf, Can Can GirlBoy Hair Candy, Extracts of Certified Organic Oatstraw, Horesetail, and Aloe, that's just off the top of my head, but what a sad list. In all those years I never found a product that was faithful; never found one to settle down with and just relax. I could never commit.

Even the latest exports from Europe couldn't pull me out of the doldrums. The most expensive hairdresser I ever used promised the world and in the end delivered very little. I wanted a hard-edged, hard-boiled, hard-arsed look, but it turned out, in the end, to be simply hard-to-manage, which in my time of grief became an obsession.

So I decided, in spite of current trends and my own apprehensions, to blow it all and shave my head. Off with the lot. Off with the Burden, the Despair, and the Agitation of ever getting the front sweep of hair just so. Off with the hopelessness of someday getting through 'that stage' and growing it past my shoulders. Away with the hope of ever again being a carefree, tousle-haired kid. And away with products.

It used to be that my lack of product commitment was eclipsed only by the promiscuity I showed towards my hairdressers—short-term relationships that started with high expectation and ended with a sense of guilt as I abandoned them and moved on. Greater and greater parts of the city became inaccessible because I was scared of running into these people who knew me so well. People who'd run their fingers through my hair, who'd held my hopes and expectations in their hands. People who'd combed out my knots when I was down, snipping away at life's dead wood, and who I, without so much as a thankyou or a goodbye, walked away from. I was embarrassed and guilty and hung my head when I walked past their salons.

Checked my blind spot and without indicating pulled out

The Toyota was bought second-hand from a beat-queen called Ezy-Neil. He'd driven it around the usual suburban mantraps with such repetition the car developed a kind of sixth gear, an uncanny ability to sniff out desperate men in need of attention, and orientated itself accordingly. On autopilot from toilet to toilet, it sniffed out victims waiting for what Ezy-Neil called 'counselling'.

Ezy-Neil was a fag on purpose. Piercings, Freedom Rings, a black leather belt, his t-shirt and tractor tyre work boots confirmed him as a relic of a time not yet passed. He wore his acid-washed jeans pulled so high and so tight his penis was forced to one side of the seam beneath the zip. It displayed itself like a vacuum-sealed vegetable at the supermarket. After his bad peroxide job it was the first thing you noticed.

Neil was named after the Ezy-Kneel apparatus, which helps people with arthritic knees get up and down in the garden. He earned the name, of course, because he was easier than the Saturday night girls in the disco lounges of the pubs on the High Street, but also because he spent a good deal of time on his knees on cold concrete floors, and in the winter they gave him trouble. No end of trouble with those knackered knees.

'Did my volunteer work today,' he'd say, blathering as usual at the bar about the day's conquests. 'She was waiting at the urinal for counselling, poor thing, pure Taylors Lakes, mind you, so what could I do?' His lips pursed and pouted as he excreted the details in bouts of excited shivers and uncontrolled twitches.

He'd say things like 'Love, she was a mess,' or, 'Oh, tragic, Love, but I set her on the right path.' Even when he scored his ultimate prize, a tough, straight-acting man (for which he claimed his counselling tools were best suited) he'd still speak of him using feminine pronouns. 'Gosh Honey, she was a butch number, you shoudda seen her, a right rough bitch.'

Ezy-Neil loved his counselling and he'd saved many guys at the end of their tether doing it. Saved a few marriages too. On his knees he did what he could for the community. It was his civic duty and he was proud of it.

After purchasing the Toyota I hardly even had to turn the wheel to end up a seasoned beat-queen too. That's what I am now. When it comes down to it, a beat-queen who loves the hunt. Loves the chase. That's what I've become.

With a plastic Catholic Jesus Blu-Tacked to the dash rather than the bobbing Elvis that was all the rage, it was on with the hunt. I drove the car to the places I knew I could find solace, and to others I guessed at. In some I read the lonesome messages on the grey toilet walls. In others I smelt the dank, stale air and searched the floors for signs of action missed. In others still, I splashed water on my face and drank from the tap-—me with a mouth like a dry fuck after too many champagnes and Stuyvys at the pub on a Tuesday night—before turning my back and walking out, glancing at a life-size cock going up an arse in Texta above the urinal.

Sometimes sex happened in the car on the stained seat covers and under the gaze of that gum-footed Jesus. It pushed home how little life changes. History stalked me, niggling and repeating, with Jesus or God or the family or whoever looking on, and as usual going, 'Tut-tut', as I lost myself with men as empty and unknown to me as I was to them, 'Tut-tut, poor old Leonard, what a shame. Look what he's up to now.'

I knew nothing more of most of the men than they were the type of guys who responded quickly when I leant over after giving them a bit of a glance and pulling up the knob of the locked car door. What more did I need to know? Over they dawdled, most showing a bit of hesitation, a bit of fear, shyness maybe, until they were in the car, and then it was double time to get the job done. The plastic Jesus with a busted fiery heart didn't give a stuff as I reversed the Christian dictum by loving the sin and abhorring the sinner. He looked on peacefully. As soon as I was done, the man in the passenger seat was out of the car. Most of the time out of my life too.

By the time Daniel spun the wheels and the troll of loneliness came to squat, I didn't care how much time I spent on the road. Anything was better than the flat. Some days I drove for hours, some days more, sometimes tailing no-one in particular, just U-turning, doubling back, sometimes reversing up next to a parked car that had driven in front ways just to get a better gander at the driver. Sometimes sitting and staring through the windscreen at the night-time ghost gums in the park. But mostly just sitting under the watchful eyes of the night sky and imagining the men who might soothe me, because sometimes what else can you do? Long nights alone with a stiffy? I trailed through a bunch of men in my mind, some with the thick black moustache and the gold neck chain of the council gardener I saw tending the hedges, some with legs (especially the calves) stolen from a passing cyclist; others with tanned, olive-skinned feet and well-trimmed toenails, the ones who'd leave sand between the sheets. With them I recalled encounters yet to come. I pressed these men together for an unlikely orgy, before, bored with the game, I did a U-turn and tried the toilet block behind the Ampol.

Jason, Shane, The Tradie, Steven, The Handbrake, Tony, they exist in every city. Men driven by hope. Propelled by a tough longing and a dumb optimism, propelled from one situation to the next, one person to the next, one vacant space to the next. They never stop searching each other out. And there's a different fella on every corner so why bother holding on? From decade to decade and from place to place they leave their mark. You'll know the sadness of these guys because of the unshed tears you'll see seeping from them in surrogate forms, and from other more willing orifices than the dried-up ducts of their eyes. You won't see tears from the tough guys I've had. A weeping sore perhaps, but tears, no, not on your nellie.

Closer back towards the city I had to lose the grief hollowing out my insides. I roamed from one small theatre of desire to the next. A knowing glance the price of admission to the impromptu spectacle that occasionally bloomed in the concrete. I roamed and I waited.

There were phone numbers too in the mess of graffiti and I wondered if those numbers ever really got rung, and if they did, who you asked for or if you just said, 'Hi, I got this number off a toilet wall ...' and waited to see what happened next. I've never rung one though. One time as a kid I copied a number down but then was too rabid with terror to make the call. But I kept that number on a small scrap of paper for years. Sometimes taking it out of my treasured-things box I made in metal work class at school. Taking it out of what was in effect a glory box for the future—my padlocked hope chest.

Sometimes I'd go for the number with a mentality of 'this is it' before chickening out when the phone was picked up. Later when I'd stayed in toilets longer than the time it took to copy a number and flee—and I suppose didn't really even need masturbation or wet dreams or any fantasies about what I wasn't getting because when you know where to look, sex is everywhere—I still picked up the number and imagined ringing. Teenagers hung off phones, making dates. Pubescent girls in cliquey groups rang shy boys: Sarah, Joanne, Deb, and sometimes me on the outer. Boys making quick perfunctory calls to girls doing homework, uneasy about small talk. Even though I never imagined homosexuals to have a life above the waist, that telephone number held the adolescent hope of ringing someone to ask him out. The school social, a Blue Light disco, a quick smoke after a Hoyts matinee—was it possible? The numbers were as precious as the digits on a rabbit's wee foot, that you rub for good luck, wishing yourself into something else. Wanting something better.

Back home I reread the letter Dan left when he came to do the clear out.

> You said you wouldn't back out on us. Now that I'm leaving, you'll probably kid yourself that you kept your word. You didn't. We could have made it. I was sure of it the moment I bought you that first Southern Comfort and we danced. Five years is a long time to practice but you're giving up just as we're getting to the good bit, getting some traction. It could have been a triumph.
>
> You said, 'Start as you mean to finish.' I guess in a way you have: you fucked me the night we met, and now you've fucked me again. But this time it was a dry painful fuck, which I guess you must have enjoyed. Me, I could have done with a little more consideration.
>
> You won't hear from me now for a while. No doubt, you'll think I'm off in a corner somewhere licking my wounds, or even contemplating the big return. I'm not. Whatever wounds I have, you're not the one to fix them.
>
> You deserve happiness. I'm not too bitter to admit that, and I guess you'll find it.
>
> Whether you can tell when it comes will be a whole other story.
>
> When you walk past the gardenia near the door think of me because of how I had to nurture it to

get the wonderful flowers it's got. Now, that's a triumph.

When you get this letter my stuff will be gone. I will say it because it's still true, I love you,

Daniel

Jason

Most of the old concrete urinals had been pulled down. They were now about as rare as the old, individual porcelain ones you only occasionally saw below the pavement of the CBD, lined up like old soldiers waiting for inspection. The toilets in parks had been replaced by more modern constructions, which, in their latest incarnation try to obliterate mischief by keeping the internal spaces open to an outside gaze. With the doors of the cubicles cut down to size any four-legged mutations are easily revealed when the undercover cops do their rounds.

Even so, some of the toilets of the inner city had escaped the shake down. The elderly wrought-iron pissoirs dotting the streets and the tiled underground chambers of the CBD were pretty much untouched by bureaucratic fingers. It was the suburban toilets, the toilets like the concrete and brick one he now walked towards— seedy, rundown—which had been cleared away. A history gone. A heritage wiped clean. You just didn't see these much any more.

It also had to be said that you didn't smell them that much anymore either. After all, it was the smell he remembered most. Or anticipated most. That's what hit him after he entered the toilet. The pungent, dank smell of piss upon piss over the decades as he walked past the barely visible MEN in flaked-off paint on the wall, and entered the architectural relic.

Jason was busting. It had been a long drive in peak hour traffic. He went straight to the urinal, stepped onto the concrete plinth, undid the buttons of his fly, pulled out his penis, sighed, and pissed. A long, satisfying piss. The muscles in his bum and the ones at the top of his legs relaxed. His feet went heavy and his back slouched. His shoulders dropped, his sphincter slackened. He closed his eyes momentarily and thought, really, of nothing. Just enjoyed the sensation and the relief.

When he'd finished he did up his fly and stepped down from the plinth, looked around the ageing space, breathed in and remembered. He looked behind the wooden cubicle door, bending his head to see if there was any writing on the wooden slats, any sign of life in the old corpse. There was nothing. Nothing written that would indicate any sign of passion whatsoever. Nothing on the door and nothing on the walls.

A piece of tin nailed over the middle part of the door was perhaps the only contradiction to the functional, unadulterated environment. Perhaps before its last drab refurbishment this small durable space had a peephole.

Now there was nothing to see, no eye pushed up to the door, no men at the urinal, no surprised schoolboy who, when he realises he is being watched doesn't move, caught like a bunny in the glaring awareness of his own desires.

Jason didn't move either. There was no hurry. He had nowhere he needed to be, and a few places he was actively avoiding. He had time on his hands. He looked at the skew-whiff toilet seat, the cistern shaped like an old metal toolbox above it, the knob of the flusher. How many arses had sat here? How much shit had been flushed down those pipes; how much toilet paper expelled into the sea?

The water in the bowl was clear. He turned away. A small sink opposite the cubicle, dirty, no soap, and a lonesome tag graffitied above it. The tag was a threat, an indication of a younger generation he didn't quite get. It held a toughness, a kind of in-ya-face ballsy attitude that the fags didn't have. Sure, they bucked the law in just as aggressive a way as the spray-painting kids, but they did it with shame rather than attitude. They'd cower rather than fight if their presence was questioned. Nod, cringe, be polite, apologise, flee. To Jason, the tag meant *I'm here and I'm here to stay. Oh, and by the way, Fuck You.*

He looked at the walls around him. The cracked lines of plaster spread in a crazed pattern like a map of unnamed streets and unremembered places. He traced one of the thicker cracks to an exposed cluster of pipes on the wall; he followed them until they disappeared into the concrete floor. The building's subterranean skeleton, he figured, was much the same as the crazed map on its surface, pipes connecting to pipes connecting to pipes and spreading like couch grass run amok. Even though this was a sexless bog in the North, it linked him to a lifetime of bodies, to a truckload of men standing with their cocks in their hands at the urinal, their feet going heavy, a slouch of satisfaction as they pissed. He figured it linked him to a network of history and to all the other pipes and cisterns that, over time, had drained away the city's scum. He was caught in a network designed to deal with waste, a network woven from pipelines and sewers and urinals and s-bends and cisterns and dirty basins and the men who used them. It made him feel less alone. It was a safety net that broke his fall. He breathed it in.

Other than the sheet of tin covering the back of the cubicle door and the tag above the sink, the only other sign that the bog had not been completely abandoned was a yellow fit tin on the wall interrupting his space and a sign above it saying *Needles Here*.

Unkempt grass fingered the struggling foundations and the cracked path. He walked back across the oval thinking three things. One, the car needed petrol. Two, he was low on money. Three, what an idiot he'd been to waste the petrol he had driving to a toilet block so far from home. What a moron. He should've just stayed in the area he knew, the area closer to home. He should have cruised the chain of beach beats that dotted the Peninsula at least as far as Beaumaris, like he usually did. He should have saved time. Saved petrol. Saved the disappointment of spending an afternoon alone and not hooking up with anybody.

At his usual cruising grounds at least he was sure of others cruising too. Even if there was no-one he wanted or no-one who wanted him, at least he knew more or less what to expect. He drove those roads with familiarity. Returning from work, going to the shop for smokes, doing the grocery shop late on Thursdays, just cruising by—rejection in his familiar world didn't dig in, and he could let it go. He could handle it.

New trade was flattening out though. Not much potential talent. Routine had settled in and nothing new or unexpected had happened in weeks. Same-old, same-old, he thought: the same cars and the same men, the same furtive glances from some and the same nods of recognition from others. He was bored. He'd driven north in search of a blip on the horizon of his mundane day. He was also thinking about toilets he'd used long ago. The smell of urine-sodden concrete reminded him. The olfactory jolt carried him back, like the bitey, acidic smell of paint stripper, it went up his nose and exposed what had been neatly lacquered over: memories of the toilets at primary school and the long stinking stretches of urinal at the footy games he went to with his dad. He was thinking of the kid he once was, the kid he tried hard to repel, then, now. But mostly, Jason was shitty about the petrol, about the waste.

He reached his car. He unlocked the door. He fastened his seatbelt, lit a cigarette, and turned the car back towards the city.

Joe

He was about to crack and show it all. All the terror, the embarrassment, the desire, the passion, and the anxiety that had been concealed for years was in danger of spilling out under neon light, erupting right there in the club. The guy was loaded with emotion, both barrels packed and cocked.

He couldn't pretend he knew how to be among these men and it was written all over his face. Sure, he was young, inexperienced, wet behind the ears, letting his hair do its own haphazard thing—no product or pretensions—just the ticket in such a jaded environment. He was bound to be snapped up in next to no time. But the anticipation had him in ribbons. Who would have the guts to risk showing their own desires by pulling him out of the limelight? Which one of the regulars, the queens lining the walls like medieval panelling, would have the balls to throw caution to wind and chuck him a lifeline? Which stale antiquity with a bleeding heart and an aching weather-beaten cock would risk a quiet uneventful Tuesday night and a mope home alone for triumph, for just one touch, or more, before this dazed kid came to and then fled? Who would take the shameful punt on him not being able to say no? After all, it wasn't a matter of who the kid wanted, of him making a choice; he didn't know what he wanted and it showed. Scared witless. This is what whoever went in for the catch was counting on. They counted on a piece of clueless virgin arse too scared to say boo, and with gay etiquette as absent as Naired hair. Really, so over-ripe he was falling rather than needing to be plucked, a gimme.

Following the old adage about being in the company of queens, the permanent fixtures kept their backs to the wall, and no-one made a move. Maybe seeing his first tentative steps into the secret world was too startling and painful to witness; a reminder of how there are no such things as queer trainer-wheels, no-one to ease your new beginnings into the world for you. A tranny just starting out might have low heels or a teen bra padded with tissues to get her going, but she only got to that point by being faced with an enormous downhill slope, perching her boy-pussy on the edge, holding her breath, and going over. She did it her way, and now so would he. He would have to fumble his way through.

He was a spectacle at the bar. His rudderless solo excursion through a sea of bodies leaving the punters who looked on frozen between amnesia and past humiliations. They stopped; they turned and looked; they had moments of recognition, but no-one went near him. No-one wanted to go back to the place where wounds are still fresh, and where coming out is never enough to disentangle you from the anguish of the closet. The pain of it still able to suck you back. They wouldn't go there even for a minute. Not even for a piece of pliable meat, a virgin opportunity, a taste of unsullied flesh. Each man expected and hoped

26

(while secretly wishing the reverse) that another would be the first to advance, the first to test the icy waters of fear and rebuttal. But nobody did. Who would have the balls to come through for him, to touch this kid and prove that the long wait had not been in vain?

Theo

The new kid wore his moccasins, the old pair his mother bought him from the Footscray market, like a trophy from the west, one of the few things he'd grabbed the night they kicked him out.

At the clubs in the Eastern suburbs, he wore his tracksuit pants with the same bravado, conscious of how the loose fit accentuated his penis and made heads turn. Conscious of a growing sex appeal he'd never before had the space to notice.

Tuan

'It was at that moment that he appeared from nowhere and swept me to higher ground,' said a man who'd waited twenty-five long, well-behaved years.

I will take the risk

He was killed in the park up the street from our house. Not near the toilet block where you might expect, where men stand around with their hands in their pockets—waiting—but on the other side of the park near the tennis courts. It happened behind Court Two, the court with the mangled wire. An early morning jogger discovered the body.

I saw the gruesome shape of the blue tarpaulin the police used to cover the corpse as I went past on the bus to school. I was thirteen. The body underneath must have been a mess. I looked out the bus window when it stopped at the traffic lights opposite the courts. A man walking his dog looked too. He pushed up against the tape marking out the crime scene. The wind curled up the edges of the tarp. His dog strained on the lead. I couldn't hear from the bus but I saw the dog growl as a policeman approached to move them on. I saw its little terrier jowls go up and I saw its little white teeth. And its owner tugged on the lead, turning the dog away.

Dental records were used to identify the body even though the victim's teeth were pretty much all gone. Later it was found that two young men had used heavy metal rods to bash him, after, it was alleged, he had tried to pick one of them up. They couldn't handle what it meant to be wanted by another man. They both freaked and each just happened to have a metal bar on hand to defend his manhood, to defend his honour. They just happened to be walking in a well-known cruising area after dark with metal rods. Just in case.

'We went crazy, out of control. It just happened,' they told the judge. I read it in the papers when the case came to trial. This was before killing a fag had been officially sanctioned through the whole 'homosexual panic defence' thing. Nevertheless, the lawyers argued that the come-on had so frightened these heterosexual men that their violent overreaction was the only way to resolve the meltdown it caused them to have. He was killed in self-defence. The murderers were treated with the full leniency of the law.

Back then, as now, it was open season on homosexuals.

The bashing and murder happened close to where another gay man had been murdered a decade earlier—the-fag-in-the-fridge-in-the-funny-house killing. It was becoming a pretty infamous part of town. Not because it was particularly dangerous or because nasty gangs hung out there. There was no excess of neon light to blaze down on the faces of working girls or street kids. There was no twinkle or haze. It wasn't Hindley Street. It was really a pretty part of town, just outside the south-eastern corner of the city's square mile. Nice. But in Adelaide you don't have to be in a seedy neighbourhood to find yourself in trouble. It can happen anywhere. City, country.

The Beaumont Children, Doctor Duncan in the river, The Truro Murders, The Family, The Snowtown Murders, not to mention the numerous others murdered across the land, across time. South Australia is fertilised with bodies in hastily dug pits. Bodies in shallow graves. Flowers grow out a kid's arse. Sour sobs out of an ear. A clump of spinifex grass from a nostril. Forget-me-nots seed themselves between a young girl's legs. The whole state is pale with murder. It should be cordoned off. Crime scene tape wrapped around its borders and tied like a big ribbon: a gleaming present with a tight bow. White picket fences, high hedges, verandas with iron lace and creeping wisteria, and the respectability of 'free settlers', the flimsy veneer, the wrapping. But it only takes the lightest fingernail scratching to expose the grime underneath. The Adelaide dirt, grey, lifeless, dry.

As kids, we always said, 'That's where that man was murdered,' as we went past the ultra-modern house where his death had occurred. Our parents had given us just enough information to nourish a much bigger tale. They told us the man was a homosexual, which, really was enough on its own, but a murder and a body dumped in a fridge! It was fascinating, fantastic. The information made even a glance at the house titillating and dangerous. We all looked at it as we went past in the car on our way to the city and nudged each other and giggled.

I imagined the body inside a square freezer with a lift-up top, the kind Granny called an ice chest. The freezer never had anything else in it. No fish from the holidays at the beach. No ice cream. No frozen peas. Just a body that didn't quite fit. Beige pants and black shoes sticking out the top.

I never regarded the dead man as a victim. He was a homosexual. Perhaps like the wicked witch that Hansel and Gretel pushed into the furnace, getting her fat kiddy-killing arse through the oven door, he deserved it—like the men who gave Doctor Duncan the final shove no doubt said, he was pushed in for our own good.

'Never trust a man in white shoes,' Mum said to me one day as we walked past the toilets in the park, and somehow, even though the feet hanging out of the fridge had (in my imagination) black shoes on them, I knew this warning was connected. I knew it counted.

As much as I could imagine the body in the freezer, and the freezer in the kitchen, and imagine the hallway leading from the kitchen to the bedroom, and imagine the bed, and two men on it, I couldn't conceive of the murder or the murderer. Maybe I was too young, too intoxicated by the fresh Adelaide air. Maybe he just fell in as he tried to prise free the last frozen chop from the ice on the bottom. Perhaps while cleaning he slipped on the wet floor and tumbled headfirst into the defrosting freezer. But the killing of a man in our neighbourhood I couldn't yet conjure up. It was a primal scene I'd keep tucked away for later. It was a way of preserving the innocence of two men screwing on a bed, a way of sorting the dread from the desires I couldn't contain or understand, a way of being a boy.

Regardless of whatever mechanisms of repression were at work, it would only take a year or two before any blocks of the imagination with regard to the realities of homosexuality in a small town were given a colonic irrigation by the media and flushed out. The reporting of the so-called 'Family Murders' in Adelaide left little to the imagination, and the violence came to haunt the city of churches as the local papers detailed the murders of a series of young men. The media traded in all the stereotypes, even though it was 1983 and homosexuals were beginning to claw their way towards a hint of legitimacy.

'The boy's body contained a cocktail of drugs and traces of lubricant were found on his anus' was spread across the front page of the paper. There were photos of the accused when the police finally arrested someone. I studied the photo, taken as he was led from the court ...

What traces of homosexuality are in your face? What knowledge— I would surely recognise in you but hide in myself—is behind your dark glasses? Would you spare me if I met you? Would you hold me for just a few days, keep me captive and then dump me, dazed and confused, with lubricant on my anus? I could find my way home if you tossed me out on a dirt lane in the hills. Would you know me if I hitchhiked late at night or walked near the beach or by the river? Would you recognise me in or out of my school uniform? Would you care? What is under your suit? Is your penis soft or hard? What would it be like if I touched it? What do you know of the city that I don't know yet? Can you see me now from your Yatala cell? Are you alone? I could touch you, if that's ok. I will take the risk. Tell me where to walk and I will be there. Please come alone, though. If you ask you can have me, but if you force me I will try to run. I am yours if you want me.

Evidence

It wasn't until I had my back to him and was walking quickly away that I heard him ask, 'Are you alright?'

The stranger might have cared, but I never turned around to find out. I took off as fast as I could, a power take-off driven by fear. *I am disgusting. Now I know it for sure. Now I have proof.* Gathering my shame and panic, I fled. I bundled up how bad I was feeling and headed towards the striped canvas canopy under which Mum shaded herself on the beach.

'Lennie, where you been?' she called.

The sun was hot and bright and bounced off the glassy sea. My eyes squinted. I hadn't yet caught my breath and was still in a crack between worlds as I ran to meet my brothers who were chasing each other in the shallow foam, spinning like sand flies.

They glanced my way and said nothing, noticed nothing, Richard ten and Mark twelve. I fell back in with them in an easy way. So much so I could almost convince myself nothing had happened. My body resumed its proper lithe posture in the sun, my eyes focused as best they could in the salty splash, and a precisely placed bell jar snapped tightly around a certain section of my brain. Legs worked. Life resumed.

I hadn't yet discovered masturbation when I stumbled across what happened in the toilet block beyond the low dunes that the wind rushed over, sandblasting the Esky and the beach shades as we dragged them back to the car on late afternoons. The off-shore breeze rushed me forward to the toilets.

A small man with brown hair and puffy rabbit-from-Alice-In-Wonderland-bearded-cheeks turned off the tap at the sink near the urinal, and looked my way. My thongs flapped at my heels as I passed him. He smiled. With no training I could read the intention in his smile and I reciprocated the invitation, I guess, without knowing how, because his eyes stayed on me. In slow panicked motion, I moved towards the urinal.

I look back now and see a boy in blue bathers crossing the concrete floor. He's ready to know everything. Yearning. Thinking his fantasies will translate directly into action. He's thinking he can govern the moment, and that there will be no space between what he imagines and what will happen. The naivety of a tall, pubescent child with manly legs is charming and seductive, which of course he does not know.

He was no taller than I was when we stood at the urinal. In nothing but bathers and an open shirt he stood next to me without actually pissing, and on seeing that he didn't bother with even the pretext of urination, I no longer needed to go either. His inaction alarmed me. Side by side we stood. Without reason. Without purpose. At which point an indefinable abyss opened up and beckoned me.

Standing and simply holding himself, he whispered, 'You can touch it.'

Through the door where I kept turning back to check, the sun stood its ground also.

The stranger held the backs of my legs to push me forward to his mouth. He felt them shake and knew their collapse as they crumbled towards his chest. My knees fell forward. Big hands on the back of young thighs.

He held me and looked up into my fourteen-year-old face. The fibres of my body went berserk with conditioned responses, ears, nose, eyebrows, elbows, knees, ankles, all parts fired up. Run, they screamed, run now and keep running—fast as hell—but instead they short-circuited and gave in. The stranger held me up when my legs stopped being much use to me.

Did he know I was fourteen? Was my age written on my body? Could it be seen in the way I walked, felt in how my skin felt? Was I a son, a boy, a student, a man, even? How did he see the fourteen-year-old face when he looked up at it? When he took my penis into his mouth, which, because of its ravenous intensity, I feared might devour me completely—my sprouting knots of pubic hair fraternising with the hair across his top lip when he pushed in close—how old was I then? And my balls, still close to my body like children not yet ready to stray too far from their mother's side, what about when he pulled down on them? How old was I then, how ready?

Mirrorball

Here it comes again, my intense bewildered spell—the time when every word, every gesture, even the sun, confirms my suspicious take on the world, and hits me like missiles, like reflected light you never saw coming. I'm in bits-and-pieces. A pack of lock-jaw memories maul me and drag me down—Mum's berserk midnight turns, the boy next door with a lame leg and a foreskin, the fat lady on the corner who drank home-brew and slapped her husband about, growling, 'What you lookin' at?' as we went past on our dragsters after school. Dance. Dance. Plans of escape, travel, forty hours of sleep, suicide, another pill, each mirrored square reflecting another option. Each refraction of coloured light leaving me no closer to a solution, but gorgeous to look at. Dance.

I dragged on a smoke. It was late. Wednesday night and the club was pretty much full. Mostly men, a few women, but not enough bodies to generate the heat I wanted, the sweat, the warmth. I swung my Stuyvy around on the dance floor, not caring if it burned an arm or the sprayed-on synthetic tops on a group of boys dancing near me. Hair around me lacquered and shiny, and me proud of my shaved head. I touched my head. Raised my arms into the air. And danced. The music worked itself into a crescendo and I tried to go with it. I waved my arms and moved my legs faster. A guy near me smiled and danced closer to me. I smiled back and took a step back. I looked down and touched my head. He came closer again, parading a bravado, a sexual confidence I couldn't match. He yelled some gesture of introduction in my face and shook his chest at me in a kind of shimmy, before spinning around to rub his back against me. Dance over. I held up my hands to keep him at bay. And left the dance floor to buy a drink.

'Len, hey. How's it going?'

'Hi.'

'How's your night going?'

'Okay. This place, it never changes ... I haven't been out much lately. Haven't been dancing. You know, it goes in cycles. Sometimes you're on the raz for ages, Thursday nights, Friday nights, Saturday nights, recovery, the saunas. But I've been out of it. God, last time I saw you we were both going at it pretty hard. You're looking good though, keeping your end up?' I shouted above the music.

'You can only keep it up so long, eh? Dan not out tonight? I haven't seen you guys in ages.'

'Nah, not tonight. What's with this bloody music?'

'You want a drink?'

The barman had his bum against the back wall of the bar, facing the punters. He gave me a watered-down smile as I approached the bar. He was employed to look pretty as much as he was employed to pull beers, to mix drinks, to sell cigarettes. But he looked tired, too, working diligently to keep up the currency of desirability and mystery. Wax had been worked hard into his hair. What should have looked windswept and tussled simply looked like it had been hassled and had had enough. A small busy tuft of neck hair worked its way free from his Bonds t-shirt. At first glance his chest conjured the image of the weather-beaten hood of an old hot-rod. The matt-black curves were desired in their time, but now looked over-sized and exaggerated. The odd glint of metallic still sparkled on the old bonnet, though, harking back to the days it fired up on the strip, to the days it made heads turn. But in reality the sparkle was only lint from a careless wash caught in the UV light.

We touched our glasses together.

'Cheers.'

'Cheers.'

And already it seemed there was little more than this that I would let myself go into. Ex-lovers, unfinished business, people I don't like, friendships in various states of decay, I didn't trust that any of these people wouldn't secretly relish my fragility as I plunged back onto the scene, back into the market. Fuck them all.

'I like your t-shirt. It's cute. I hardly recognised you without your, hair. It suits you.'

I shook the ice in my glass.

'So how is Dan?'

'Alright. Fine.'

I didn't want to tell him that we were done. That I had failed.

The music by the bar was loud and made it hard to talk.

'It feels nice,' I yelled close in at his ear, touching my skull. I could've kissed him, and almost, out of a sudden sense of misplaced desire (tonight he wasn't what I was looking for) bought on by his smell, lurched forward to do so. But stopped myself.

'My head, it feels nice.'

Both of us watched the men moving around, too distracted to really care about the conversation we were in, too distracted to enter each other's world for any longer than a brief moment. What if an opportunity is missed? But I leant in and asked another question, using the chance to draw in the sweet purposeful smell of his aftershave, before walking away to stand alone. Like a trick done with mirrors, I made myself relax, made myself available.

Silence

I started being a slut, a proper adult one, late in the day—well after I'd graduated from high school. I started being an improper slut, a childish one, a good deal earlier. But because I never talked about it, the sex I had was always secret, and I felt it never happened. I was just as embarrassed to be a virgin as everybody else.

The sex education teacher mixed starch and water in a glass, whisking it fast with a spoon, really frothing it up. The fatty skin under her arms quivered as the spoon rattled against the sides of the glass. The starch was white and milky. She made everyone touch it, boys and girls. 'This is what sperm is like,' she said.

I've already been fucked ragged though, Miss. So I'll sit here quietly on my arse which has burned-flaming-anger-red leaking with blood and sperm. I've tasted the liquid you're imitating. I've been forced to drink it, and sometimes I've wanted to. I let him do it. I've had my dick in holes that are younger, older, cleaner, dirtier than the kids around me. I've met men in the park after school, and you say smoking in your school uniform will degrade the name of the school and tarnish its reputation. I've been fucked in public toilets with my school pants down and the back of my blazer up. More than once on some days. Shut the hell up about pregnancy, about abortion, about waiting. I can no longer wait. I don't have to wait. For anything. It's written on the dunny walls. You just have to be brave enough to turn up. I've waited long enough, dreaming up an orgy of spastic bodies, hands, holes, dicks, no faces, writhing like a mass of white bait or worms. Now I can have it. You're too late, Miss.

Mum tells my brothers and me that boys like to practise having sex by using a toilet roll.

'Listen boys,' she said, when Richard, Mark, and I are in the kitchen making white bread sandwiches after school. 'The girls came over for lunch and Bev was telling us about an article she'd read on boys and sex.'

Whenever there was an awkward silence, the word 'sexuality' soon fell out of someone's mouth to fill it. School classes, television, books on the topic of puberty left on the hall table at home, pamphlets handed out at school, the adults pushing information we didn't want. Mum inevitably pushed the hardest even though she never seemed comfortable in the role. Like a door-to-door salesman pushing something we hadn't asked for; but she never entirely believed her own hard-sell rhetoric, and expected to have the door slammed in her face at any moment. The alcohol she'd drunk at lunch had given her a reason to go a little harder, jam a foot in the door that wouldn't budge.

'Boys use toilet paper rolls to masturbate and to learn about intercourse'—another word she liked to use. 'Apparently some boys use butter and other kitchen spreads to masturbate with, as well,' she said. She told us this while scraping the plates and stacking the dishwasher, with her back to us. It was her own humiliating version of sex education.

We looked at each other like she'd finally lost it, and that what she was saying had nothing to do with us, which we all hoped it didn't.

Mark reached for the butter and the peanut paste to put together another sandwich. When he had a dob of butter on the end of his knife I said to him, 'Go for it, Mark, you've got the idea, that's it, a nice big dob of butter.'

'Get stuffed,' he said back.

'Watch your mouth,' was what I heard from the sink.

For the most part I grew up in a household with a strict Don't ask, Don't tell policy. I'd already transcended the toilet roll, but still I felt like a virgin because experiences are made real in language, and at home there was no room to speak of such things. It was just as well really, it served me well, providing the training ground to deal with the silence surrounding HIV and AIDS.

In the early 90s Act-Up said SILENCE = DEATH. Under the sparkling fallout of the new millennium, silence equals a hot filthy fuck—no talking, no condoms, no regrets.

It made her feel pretty

Daniel still gone, not even a call. In the kitchen the dishes are piled up high so I run them under the tap. 'Stack them and they're as good as done' is my philosophy. Me using the hotplate on a Stuyvy and a brew of coffee and this is all I need. Mandy won't give it up on the phone, yacking about a trick that screwed her ...

'Smudged my slip-dick and twisted my bonnet, fucking turd. You think I want to go down on that. A mile of curtain before you get to the stage and a plate of cheese and greens waiting in the wings. No thanks, sorry honey; I don't think so, a shower perhaps? Wouldn't take no for an answer and then turned on the rage. Fucking shit, no idea how to treat a lady. Loop-the-Fucking-Loop. Screaming at me, stomping around, scared the shit out of me. Christ, no respect. He's got a fish tank in one corner, a folded up pool table in the other, and a giant cutout of Billy Idol near the door. Fucking queen, a real bogan fucker, probably goes to the dogs. Anyway, shit everywhere, a regular fucking minefield to get out of. I made it to the door, still had my sensibles on thank God, so ran like hell.'

Trapped on the phone because Mandy was sobbing up a storm about the life she didn't choose. How all queens went to Sydney and tricking was the only thing that made her feel pretty. How The Wall was there for the boys, but she fancied a bit of lippy and a few frills and with that came a clobbering from trade or the old man. 'Every week I was roughed up, doing my face with eyes like balloons. I'm sick of it,' she said. 'I'm not as tough as I used to be. Those boys had it easy, took the safe road.'

'Took it any way they could,' I went. Mandy laughed and coughed at the same time.

Mandy had stopped street work years ago. Now she'd stopped parlour work too. She had a daytime job in a hairdressers in the plaza and a de facto brute into which she poured her dish-pan dreams. 'Time for a girl to settle,' she'd say. Wiping the sink of the tight kitchen in the tight flat—her one small domain into which The Brute wouldn't dare throw anymore of his shit—relaxed her. She was becoming the contented one at the sink, mostly. But she hadn't stopped hooking altogether, even though she saw herself finally getting out of the industry, which, because I'd heard her saying it for most of the fifteen years she'd been working, I'd believe when I saw it. Now, deep undercover, she took small, late night doses of what had once saved her from buttondown shirts, tweed shorts, knee-high woollen socks, and a long nine-to-five life. On the nights when The Brute, who sold paper supplies and sometimes took overnight trips to regional centres, was out of town, Mandy would ring one or two of the clients she'd retained over the years, or visit a new word-of-mouth fella, like she had with the Bogan Fucker. Small, late night doses of what once made her feel pretty.

Nostalgia for the life of a street walker, which can be as off as shit and as bitter as cum, but you get through. Being a bitch. Scoring gear on cold nights and blasting it quick to keep warm. Flaunting black thigh-high boots and a black mini skirt. Cruising a car with a wound-down window and baby seat in the back, letting his lies wash your honest life to the surface. Seeing the first wee buds of your hormone titties, shaving your legs, plucking two slivers above long eyelashes. Distinguishing yourself from the drag queens on the strip who'd bellow words like 'Darling' and 'Divine' in deep ballsy voices while drinking stubbies of beer with straws. Pausing to remember only the odd, occasional thing about your childhood as you blossomed on William Street: *men in gumboots are prone to violence*. Playing out the big fantasy for the dumb-fuck Johns, doing trick sex and having your tight-as-iron thighs make them gasp. Holding your ground to be a woman, not giving up cock for anything but the big, big bucks. Doing the whole Julia Roberts *Pretty Woman* thing when they take you to the Novotel or the Radisson. The raucous camaraderie of the other girls and the power of defending your turf when you graduate up the ranks. Stumbling off your sling-backs arm in arm with one of the first friends you made when you hit the streets. Pissed and plaiting your ankles on a Sunday morning walk home in the already hot summer sun, passing families heading to church in clothes of thick well-mannered fabric. Splitting the seam of your mini by squatting behind a dumpster without first hitching the skirt high enough. Being maggoted and forgetting the angle of your cumbersome and unloved thingie (she was one of those well-hung sisters), and pissing into your pulled down stockings,

47

squatting on unsteady heels. Two or three hundred bucks on an average night, once a thousand big ones. Having money to burn at lingerie shops and cosmetic counters. Giving no second thought to the tight-lipped women at the counters who snob you off. Coffee and smokes in a nice cafe, and home to sleep.

Mandy

His mobile phone is so small he has to hold it with the tips of his fingers, like the tiny precious object it is. When he holds it up to his ear you can't see it at all. It's lost in his big hands.

As she walked towards him, she thought he was squeezing a pimple on the side of his face, near his ear, and she was disgusted. She looked away.

Joe

Let's not pretend it didn't hurt. The Christmas function was something he had to do, and it was done. Floating up the Yarra on a tinselly pontoon of food and booze and drunken workmates was not his idea of a night out. Had never been.

The receptionist with the latest fake Louis Vuitton handbag tucked high under her armpit and a short leather skirt cut well above the knee, saying things like, 'You'd be such a great catch, why no girlfriend?' His boss giving the speech he usually made at staff meetings about motivation and commitment, about getting out what you put in. The only difference tonight being that the prospect of a Christmas bonus made it tolerable. It made you think maybe the job was worth it, that someone noticed the slog and cared. The other salesmen in a group on the deck gossiping. Let's face it, bitching their little hearts out; and the prospect of too much free booze turning their petty resentments into something more threatening ever present.

Joe wasn't out at work. Hammond Industries employed a particular type of guy to sell a particular type of machinery. And it was simple work. Industrial floor sanders were, on the whole, easy to off load, but at twenty-five years of age, he was sick of the lies. Even white lies and small omissions take their toll. The cover up was draining him, making him worried as he looked over the bathroom sink in the mornings, making his hair fall out too.

Joe was pissed. 'Got lots to do tomorrow, family stuff,' is what he told his workmates after the boat docked and they headed towards a pub near Flinders Lane.

At The Underground he was comfortable enough to be who he couldn't be with the blokes at work. The club was relief. No-one there cared if he was married or had a girlfriend. No-one cared if he was in or out or whatever. He was there to lose himself in the smoky fog of bodies, bodies on tap. It had been a tough week—it had been a tough night—and Joe was there to forget. Not since he was a kid had he felt free from worry. The Christmas function had reminded him yet again.

A buffed young man with swollen nipples, a cocky smile, and a red Santa's costume pulled on jackboots. His square brutish face looked down from a Tom of Finland poster high on the wall in the video lounge. Joe thought of the Christmases he'd had with his family, the excitement and the celebration. He remembered dancing rock'n'roll to the Beach Boys on Christmas day with his sister. He remembered Christmas Mass. He remembered a tall glass of Coke on a hot day. He also remembered the first time he'd gone to the sex club. As scared as he was about what he was doing and about who he might become, he remembered above all feeling impregnated with possibility. That's what was different between being at the club or at the other social functions he was expected to show his face at, Christmas parties, family do's, and increasingly, weddings and Christenings. At The Underground he was rejuvenated.

When The Tradie pulled down his pants Joe's world reduced and blacked out like it sometimes does in the movies. Accelerated zoom. Extreme close-up. Background fade. For a moment Joe focused on what was immediately in front of him without the incursions of his surroundings. Nothing else mattered. The penis was the centre of his universe. He pulled the underpants to the floor. Nothing had importance. He touched The Tradie, whose arms were hairy and whose hands were rough and dry, but with well-clipped nails. Nothing else counted. He felt the thick hair of The Tradie's behind as he pushed it forward to smother his face in the sweaty crotch. He breathed in and the feelings that had ravaged him most of the night, the feelings of being an outsider, of not belonging, the feelings that alcohol had not pushed away, loosened their grip.

He'd spent so many years trying to read and decipher the codes and clues given by boys and men that now, finding himself simply and safely exposed to the stranger's raw, inescapable proclamation of his sexuality, was overdue relief. In the club there was no second-guessing.

For a second Joe's mind turned off and red light exploded in front of his closed eyes, a dappled bliss blotting out the world of ordinary things. The hassles from Ivan at work disappeared; the landlord and up-coming house inspection vanished; the late tax return, the overdue Visa card payments, the mundane conversations he had with his father and the sister he loved, all dissolved. The Christmas party was over too.

The Tradie disappeared as well. His body remained present only insofar as it motored the penis Joe needed, the penis that was now to the back of his mouth, being pushed into his throat. The Tradie's body had no other function than to machine the tool of Joe's relief. That was it. No personalities, no worries, no arguments, no obligations. At that moment Joe dealt with his one immediate concern: what was in his face.

The relief lasted only for a minute, then time resumed and the noises around him intruded. Men shuffling about on the other side of the thin cubicle walls. Someone cumming in the next cubicle. The whirling of the overhead fans. Both men now naked. A condom packet opened. Joe rolled over by firm directive hands. Joe with eyes closed and forgetting.

Perhaps, he hoped, as he rose from the black vinyl mat in the small hot cubicle, the fraudulent crummy guy he was might be left behind. When he got up from all-fours, stretched, clicked his achy joints and blinked himself out of his stupor, would there be traces of what he was leaving behind? Would there be something more than a puddle of cooling fluids, a torn sachet of lube, some sweaty follicles of hair, a pool of dirty little lies?

As he wiped himself clean with hand towel from the dispenser and prepared to find the next man, Joe hoped the putrid mistakes he'd made in the past might keep their heads hung low, their hands folded in their laps, and remain on the mat to be wiped away when the cleaner did his rounds. He was done with them. There was a danger: if someone else used the cubicle before the cleaner made it, his old leftovers might then, being the cunning and parasitic excuses for life they were, climb onto the next occupant's back and be gone. They could exhaust someone else for a change, get under someone else's skin with their constant quibbling over right and wrong. Either way, he was done with what had become unaffordable excess baggage.

To finish the job, Joe let a bunch of men go through him. The night was a doozy. The last man he was with, himself mostly spent and so much less abrasive than the previous gang of hard fucks, was simply there to burnish the material the others had already laid. Steven, as he vaguely remembered, smooth and amyl-driven, wasn't there to shatter him (this had been achieved), but rather, to lovingly nudge him a little further from the lousy disappointment he felt he was when he stumbled away from those happy Christmas idiots six hours earlier. At just the right pace, Steven prepared him for the world outside.

Bruce in a small town

His face was swollen with humiliation as he held up the flake and let batter drip from where its tail would have been before it was filleted. Rings, earrings, bangles, barrier cream on his face to keep the greasy heat of the deep fryer from penetrating his skin, and a home-done hair colour. It wasn't appreciated in the takeaway food shop of a hick town, but he went to the trouble anyway. He kept himself looking nice, smart, clean. He ran rings around those small-town yobs, who, he reckoned, wouldn't know the first thing about style or seasonal trends. Bruce did. He bought the magazines, and as best he could, kept himself up with fashion; he could tell you when cargo pants went out and when caps came in. He was up with the transitions.

It wasn't so bad these days but it still hurt. Friday and Saturday nights were the worst. If only he could be back home watching videos or sleeping when the pub closed. If the deep fryers could be switched off, the counters wiped down, the till emptied and reconciled, and the Closed sign flipped well before midnight, he'd be safe. But Bonnie's Takeaway was his first job and he needed the money.

Hey you, cum-breath, get your pussy arse over here. Come here babe, sit on this, we're waiting for service. You sell Chiko Rolls and donuts? You, ya faggot, wanna step outside, wanna make something of it. Me and the guys wanna know why you don't come to the pub, think ya too good for us, do ya? Think ya spoof-covered shit don't stink. Not enough girls there forya. Wuss. You pussy fag, you're a disgrace. They shudda drowned you at birth.

Sorry, man, he's just had a few too many, yeah, don't worry man, come to the pub when you knock off and we'll buy you a beer. Here man, shake me hand, earn. It's cool man, it's cool. Come on, Benny, you too, shake the pussy boy's hand.

Bruce had heard it all.

He was already counting the silver when Luke, Steve, Ricko, and Darryl pushed through the door making the chimes jingle. Bruce looked up. He made a note of where he was up to with the change, snapped two moneybags shut, and slid the drawer of the till closed.

Their floppy, jovial bodies told him they were pissed. Not plastered, but well on the way. Only Darryl made eye contact, which was hard and determined, nothing new. The others gazed at the menu board as though, by a miracle, something different than what they usually ordered might spring out from the blur and take their fancy. They stared up like dazed night-gazers waiting for a shooting star. Waiting with no urgency or worry. Bruce tightened up and told himself to make his face as neutral as possible. Take the order, make the food, take a bit of shit while his back was turned, take the money, and get them out. Then home. Safe. That's what he needed to do.

As with his neighbour's unpredictable German Shepherd, he needed to be calculated, cunning. Should he avoid their eyes or take a deep breath and stare them down? What might work best? He felt the same fear and indecision when he walked past the Turner's driveway on his way home, the same fear of murderous canine instincts.

'Hi guys, what do you want?' His voice sounded high, girlie, he thought. When the words came out he blushed. He looked down at the notebook on which he would write the order. 'See ya spunk,' was written on the top of the front page. Lisa had just knocked off. By now she'd be on the dirt track near her home, probably indicating, probably turning left past the dam. Bruce was alone.

'What do you want, guys, we're closing soon.'

He knew each of them from school. Two had been in the year above him, two in his year. Luke and Steven were brothers, Ricko lived near the Hamilton turnoff, and Darryl had been suspended in Year 10 for selling dope.

'Mate, how's it goin,' said Luke, 'havin' a good night, are you? A hamburger with the lot.'

'Make it two,' added Steve.

Then Ricko went, 'three.'

'A Coke as well, mate,' Steve went, and Ricko echoed, 'me too, mate, make it two.'

The bangles rattled as Bruce wrote down the orders. His hands felt clammy.

'You want anything,' he said to Darryl, who still had a hard, set expression on his pimply face; still more than any of them reminding Bruce of the flea-bitten German Shepherd.

When Darryl looked at him, Bruce took a quick shallow breath. Not being tough or rugged or outdoorsy in a small country town had sharpened his instincts. Not being able to kick a football in a straight line had taught him to sniff out danger at twenty feet. He was ready.

'Minimum of chips.'

Darryl looked Bruce straight in the eye and then added, 'Bruth.'

'Minimum of chips, Bruth,' he said, accentuating the lisp, and the other guys sniggered, the way children laugh at dirty jokes.

The pen had sweat on it. Bruce wrote down the order without looking up. Then fumbled one after the other as he took their money and counted back the change. His face went red, red, redder. An electric spark passed through the five-dollar note that he and Darryl touched at the same time as he paid for the chips. When Bruce gave him the change, not bothering to count it back, he said it again, 'Thankth Bruth.'

Fat spat when he flipped the burger patties. The bacon sizzled and the exhaust fan rumbled, but he thought he heard someone say, 'Wait for him outside.' He thought he heard someone say, 'Bruth.' He thought he heard the word 'fag', and he thought his legs felt a bit like jelly. He lifted the egg on top of the pattie and on top of that put the cheese, bacon, and onion. Three small stacks that could be lifted onto the rolls with the paint scraper he was sent to buy from the Thrifty in the main street on his first day at the job. He lifted the chip basket out of the oil, jiggled it, and dunked it back. He was careful not to let the oil spit at his hands because he hated how much got into his rings, especially into the clawed setting of the amethyst he'd scored on a shopping trip to Melbourne. He was careful and methodical. He took a breath in and yelled out, 'Chicken salt on those chips?' without turning around. And Darryl said, 'Yeth'.

Bruce lined up the grease-proof paper and opened three brown bags. He completed the hamburgers with tomato, beetroot, and lettuce. On top of that went tomato sauce and mayo. He'd taken a lot of shit in his eighteen years, and had rarely given much back. As far as he could remember he'd never been encouraged to fight. His mother would say things to soothe him. 'Turn the other cheek, honey.' And, 'It takes more guts to walk away than to start a fight.' Things like that. So that's what he usually did. He turned the other cheek and sometimes ran. And his father? He loved Bruce. They loved the cows and the sheep on the farm. They loved working together on a Saturday afternoon, crutching, worming, delivering a breech birth calf. His father didn't believe in violence either. Bruce had never been encouraged to fight. Never encouraged to punch first and ask questions later.

He looked over his shoulder. Steve, Luke, Ricko and Darryl were standing near the door. Steve was half-out having a smoke, Ricko was drinking a stubbie. The other two were slapping each other about and laughing. Bruce had his back to them. He looked around one more time. They were in their own Vic Bitter and Bundy world.

He worked his tongue forward from the back of his throat like a front-end-loader gathering dirt. He pulled some muck down from his nose to his throat, and then worked the throat muscles to bring it into his mouth, all with only the slightest noise. The chips were ready so he leant left and hooked the lip of the cradle over the catch to let the chips stand and drain. He held the glob of warm spit in his mouth while he looked back at the guys to check, but needn't have bothered. The tomato sauce and mayo dripped through the shredded lettuce and the melting butter penetrated the top of the toasted rolls, which were as thirsty as a Wettex.

He only had spit for two hamburgers. But that was enough.

Bruce salted the chips and wrapped the burgers before sliding them into the brown bags. Once again Darryl was the only one to give him attitude as they collected the food, made their grunting noises, and jostled each other out the door.

It was 12.35 when Bruce flipped the sign on Bonnie's Takeaway. The car was parked on the other side of the street. He could see it. It was a clear run. He had the keys ready. It was an hour later when he arrived home, shaken but not hurt, and flicked on the telly. *Rage* was on. It was a typical Saturday night.

Bruce gone

When he was finally forced out, he couldn't believe he didn't go earlier. He just couldn't imagine getting out. For him it was unthinkable, not yet a possibility. No-one told him how easy it would be. How hard can it be to pack a bag and turn your back? He was nineteen, after all. It was the usual escape to the big city story. The small idling town conspired to keep him trapped, and for too long he'd listened to its gurgling fictions. He purged his disappointment and anger in the glare of city lights. Nhill, Wagga Wagga, Kempsey, take your pick, any regional piss-hole had the same effect. It produced the same resentment, the same unremitting bruise. It produced another proud queen.

Love

Me with sad eyes in the day room. Only walking through on my way to visit the old girl on the upper level. Chairs arranged in huddled bunches. Arranged like feisty bits of chitchat were already full-blown and a fat arse on anti-Ds plonking itself down would be a real conversation killer. Cards and dominoes set up on a table in the centre of one group. Tattered old cases and missing bits. I just walk. One foot, then the next, then the next. Eyes sodden behind with tears but never flooding the cheeks. It was a top-shelf downer, the whole pastel place. But with the nurses geeing it all along, you didn't want to be the one to burst the bubble. In the hospital no windows opened and the air was thick with the smell of apple crumble and Ajax.

I wanted to smoke, but there was only the small courtyard with white plastic furniture and a tub of sand for the snuffed-out butts. And it was grim work. Usually a few people standing around, the visitors talking loud about the outside, talking up which side they were on. Anyway, this day I was plugged into the Walkman and kept walking. I'd smoke later.

The music from *Ryan's Daughter* was in my ears. A find for Mum I'd bought in a junk shop. I'd only seen the movie once as a kid but Mum played the soundtrack over and over. One time she cracked me on the nut for skidding the needle across the record. She cared about that music heaps, said, 'You die when you hear it.'

The movie's a story of love gone wrong, which even as a kid I understood. Love that shouldn't happen because you're just pushing shit up hill the whole time to keep it. Love that everyone's against, and you can do nothing but give up when they run it out of town. The music rolls like the waves pounding the fishing village where the movie is set, waves of sadness that are wet and soft and hurt. Like when you cry and it's painful but you feel better, a bit cleaner, after. I clicked off the Walkman and decided against giving it. All those memories and if it still makes her want to die, the doctors and nurses won't be happy since it's all hands on deck and round the clock just to get her to tomorrow. Maybe it was best dead and buried.

Mum's room was on the second floor of the old wing. I didn't take the lift. Just followed the line on the wall where the light chuck-coloured green above meets the dark chuck colour below. Newly painted, but with an old theme—70s government building paint job, the same as at the dole office and the TAFE. Follow the line long enough and all the shit-hole places for the down-and-out would join up. One long line that's really a circle because you're chasing your tail if you think a week in the nut house, a handout of two hundred a week, or a night class is going to pull you up.

Over the years I'd seen enough of the twisted remains from occupational therapy to last a lifetime, even a short one. If I never again saw another uneven pinch pot or a fabric covered coathanger it wouldn't be too soon. For my twelfth birthday she'd given me a macrame pot plant hanger made in a hospital class, and nothing else. No clothes. No bike. No swap cards.

She handed it to me with a smile, me feeling sure the present would be what I wanted, even though I hadn't expected much and had no picture of what it might be. It was squashy in the wrapper, hard in parts, soft in others. I turned it over and shook it. My brothers smiled in expectation too, 'Happy birthday Lennie.' Everybody smiled at the wrapping on my twelfth birthday.

More than anything, though, more than anger and more than disappointment, I felt embarrassed. The gift was a sign of my own failings and had to be kept quiet, so I told no-one about the plant hanger Mum made in the nut house and gave me for my twelfth birthday.

'Carn, old girl,' I said, real gentle as I helped her up from the bed where she sat. 'Let's go out for a smoke, get you some fresh air.' Out of it and wobbly on her feet, her comprehension two paces back as we shuffled along the carpet. This time taking the lift down to the ground floor, which was large enough for a wheeled in bed, but we were the only two standing on the huge descending square of linoleum. Not speaking even though I wanted somehow to blow apart the silence. Past pastel prints, Monet, Renoir, McCubbin, the usual gang. Through the sliding doors. Back to where Mum usually sits on the plastic furniture in the corner of the green trellised enclosure, back to the tub of sand and the permanent acrid smell of the snuffed-out butts. I lit two Stuyvys and passed one to her.

Another odd couple smoking. Her with scars running between her wrist and her elbow. Neat, ordered, and old. Him, like me, in from the outside. Her with black clothes, black hair, and a metal bat with its wings spread hanging on a leather thong around her neck. Her boobs low and pale, stretch marks running parallel to the taut ribbing of her v-necked black top. Her a Goth staring at nothing. Him like me, content to start at the crotch and work from there as we give each other the once over. Him well groomed. Expensive engineered denim cuffs touched up suede runners. Fresh t-shirt material stretched between two pumped pecs. Her brother maybe. He looked away when our eyes meet, looked straight past me, through me, over me. Summed me up and dismissed me with his cold firm stare. The kind of stare that takes in everything, that can work a room in next to no time, locating the most handsome man in a crowd and assessing the most dangerous, which, in this hostile and horny city might be one and the same thing.

Fuck it, I thought, and unashamedly looked at the denim-covered package between his legs.

Mum just sat. Her hair blowing up in the back-teased layers created by the hospital hairdresser a few days earlier. Dry, brittle, thinning hair. Occasional small words into the wind, the odd arbitrary question, so ill-placed you wondered where it came from. What synapse fired to make her say, 'Is Mark married yet?' when how much we disliked his wife was the one thing we all still agreed upon?

Mum out of her slippers and back in bed. All bed clothes pulled up and the old rug over her feet, the one we'd picked burrs from after picnics. The one that Mum had spread out while dad was breaking up twigs and setting the paper. The one that could fit two adults, three kids, the salads and the chops on when we were all under ten. The rug that here, in the ward, made me want to give dad a good kick in the arse. It was one of the few things she'd brought over to make Melbourne a home after he'd upped and left her. To do his own thing.

For more than twenty years the two of them together. Solid. The same good house with a pool. A caravan in the park at Yorks. The summer. All good for near twenty-five years. 'Mad as a cut snake, you're off your bloody rocker, round the Mary Lou, she's dead from the neck up,' is some of what he mumbled after, I suppose, 'Til death us do part and I do.' Until in the end, 'I'm just worn out, I've had enough,' then finally, nothing. He mowed the lawn, clipped its edges, wiped down the catcher, returned the mower and the petrol tin to the shed and one Sunday left.

Two small pictures on the nightstand: one with all five of us and the dog and the shining Commodore in 81; the other, Nan and Pop all dressed up and being proper in a blue frame. A few bobby pins and a china figurine of a long-haired dog are there too.

Her hand held in mine. I kissed her hand, kissed the fingers, kissed the smoke. Leant forward and kissed her face.

'See you soon Mum, Thursday probably.'

'Hopefully this time, Len, hold your breath. The doctor says things could look up from here. Maybe the next round of treatment will work.' She crossed her fingers and lifted her hand a centimetre or two off the blankets. She tightened her face in lieu of a smile.

One. Two. Three. I counted to three and then looked back. Bingo. So did the guy I'd seen when we were smoking.

'You can tell a fag every time,' Stolly Philosopher On Life had instructed not long after we'd met and he was giving me advice about cruising. 'After the first look, look away, count to three, and look back. If the guy's still looking, you're on. It's as easy as that. A poof always gives himself away.'

One. Two. Three. I was cruising.

He looked back twice more before we got to the men's toilet opposite the reception desk. My heart thrashed about as it had when I was a clueless kid at the beach. The fear and anticipation of a pick-up never lessened. The hope that somehow, in the end, it would make a difference is what diminished.

I avoided the nurses' eyes and trailed the faded denim pockets into the small, clean hospital toilet. 'Hey,' I said, soft and tired, a tender tone in my voice, a voice I didn't recognise for cruising. At the urinal we looked at each other for a second longer than we had with cigarettes in hands outside. Still only glanced, him just as much as me urgent to fuck with the tranquillised libido of this place. Each dry pull on the other's penis gave us back what mental hospitals like this had stripped from guys like us over the decades. But in the end, it wasn't enough. What touch would be rough enough, hard enough, to hold back what might gush out? Nothing could be rampant enough to make me forget or help me to feel nothing.

I looked into his eyes and blushed, but held my gaze. We both blushed. Long dark lashes framed a distant life— a life not to be shared here, a secret life of hurts I could easily guess at. In his face I saw my own fear and sadness. But mostly what I saw was been-there-done-that, and the strain of the day. We pulled at each other in the usual dalliance of power where two men are deciding who will submit to whom and how they will proceed to the next step. Deciding without words, staring each other down, until one submits, or they both walk away.

Fuck the middle ground. I needed either to dominate or be dominated, thoroughly. And I needed him with his hands on me to make the decision.

I pushed his hand away from my penis. It wasn't going to happen. I wasn't like Ezy-Neil. I couldn't counsel him. I had nothing to offer. I was spent. He'd have to take charge of me and it was clear he couldn't. I tucked myself back into my pants, touched his shoulder and smiled. I looked into his face and decided to hold my misery rather than spurt it at the hospital walls I despise. I said, 'Let's leave it, mate.' And I walked out.

Hitting gear

Under the sheets, under the mattress, under the bed, and then under the rug. Even the floorboards, if he'd had an axe, would've got the once over, I'm sure of it. With rage and urgency his fist went through the bedroom window and as clear as day the money wasn't stashed behind that. Rent money we'd needed badly, for the rent. The fist went through. 'Just you give me the money now, one small cunt of a taste is all I need. That's all I'm asking for. Please,' he begged, until I said, 'Give it up, for God's sake Daniel. NO. For the last fucking time, NO!' And then he was off again. Hand running along the metal pelmet of the Venetians leaving blood, flapping out magazines and the pages of books. Ripping and smashing to get behind the jars in the kitchen too. More broken glass. 'Fuck you, just give me the money. I can't go through this again. Twenty-five dollars for a taste. Fuck. Please. Now. For the last time, one fucking cap, I promise. Now. Please.' Plain and self-raising flour onto the floor. Cornflakes and flapjacks. Shit from arsehole to breakfast time. Jam, vegemite, cans of tomatoes, split peas, vanilla essence, everything we had on the shelves, which wasn't much, turned out because I said No. He went at our small stockpile like a dog digging a hole, ferociously scraping away with his paws. Soap, toilet paper, more cans, brown sugar, choc bits, everything past his mangy hind legs and onto the floor.

Twenty-five dollars was enough on Smith Street before they cleaned up Collingwood and drove the problem into someone else's backyard. Twenty-five dollars was enough then for half a Collingwood cap.

Daniel out of it in the stairwell behind Safeway. It wouldn't happen again on my watch.

All the dry goods except expensive Macadamia nuts spewed onto the lino. If he started at the fridge next and dumped the milk and butter and eggs, we might have a near complete recipe for my famous double-choc Brownies there on the floor, add this, take that. When smack entered the house, creeping in to do what smack does, and turned our lives upside down, I would've gladly made them too. I would gladly have him get the munchies and beg me how he sometimes did, 'Gowarn, baby, make the brownies, gowarn.' I missed him having the plain and simple, easy to deal with munchies, which never ended up with fists cut from shattered glass, and which we sometimes shared together.

Him on the nod I couldn't stand. Daniel drooping on the couch, his head on a loose sprung neck, his eyes rolled shut, as action-packed as a fart in a bottle. Totally out of it. His mouth open but nothing coming out. There on the couch like a sack of shit, which once I loved, still loved, and which smack had stolen and eloped with into a world of daytime telly. Whooping it up with Jerry or Oprah or Judge Judy. All day long with sisters-who-fuck-their-brothers-who-are-trannies-in-secret-who-have-a-bastard-son-who-married-a-knife-wielding-granny-for-her-money, maybe. All day long with tell-it-like-it-is Phil with the tough love, and Judge Judy awarding nothing to the plaintiff because she's a single black Mum without a job who didn't try hard enough to raise good kids. Hour after hour of daytime TV washing over him. Then again maybe nothing. Perhaps he didn't hear a peep from the telly, being as deaf as a trussed-up gimp with candle wax cooling in his thumping ears and cigarette burns up and down his inner thighs. Perhaps he'd drifted off to a world like that, far, far away. But how would you ever know once those eyelids rolled down, rattling closed like shopfront rollerdoors in a bad neighbourhood.

'Heroin isn't evil, you just have to take the upper hand,' said Mandy. 'You have to catch yourself before it devours you.' She could take herself right to the edge and always find her way back, that was Mandy. She never went over. But she had no sympathy for Daniel, who was, as far as she was concerned, as good as useless. She called him a smack-freak and a junkie. 'Cut the cord and move on,' was all she said when I told her about the kitchen and the window. Eventually, in the end, after I'd demanded it, she listened. She listened to me telling her I wouldn't leave, and for two more long years I kept to my word.

On Smith Street I asked around. 'You chasin? You chasin? Wanna get on?' was the response to any eye contact as I approached those I reckoned might know where Dan was. A woman with a child in a pram asked for two dollars and

I ignored her. A child ate a chocolate bar while his dad said, 'Stay there. Don't move a muscle,' so he stayed put, alone on a shop step, stillish but for the biting at the chocolate. 'My wallet, he's got my wallet,' yelled a guy with shopping bags in both hands, and two undercover Ds came from nowhere and set chase. I only cared to have Daniel home. Probably I'd give a lecture and the silent treatment in the car but then me at rest when he slept it off in bed. Me then doing the clean up, taping up black plastic to cover the window, sweeping the floor quietly.

I looked there, but he wasn't near Safeway or the bins behind it. Where? Standing, laying down, with a group of people who'll make it fun and games to get him back, make it the devil's own job to take him? You chasin? You chasin? And in a way I was. I wanted. I couldn't wait. Maybe by the ANZ or further up Gertrude Street towards the city. Maybe in a coffee shop and straight. Men around a soup van were making a ruckus that warded me off. Where? I crossed the road to check the lane behind the National Bank. Somehow it was my fault. That's what I felt; that if I was in some way better, someway more, enough, then I could stop him getting on, make him decide that the last nudge was the last nudge. That we ourselves, the two of us, were all we needed. But there was always the next taste. Maybe not for a while, not straight away at first. But in the end I would find that's where he'd been when he was home late from work, or just didn't bother to go. So in the end I blamed myself, telling myself that the two of us were good for nothing, and he was up to God knows what because of it.

Family

Daniel was a clean-freak. Sometimes twice a day washed, scrubbed, loofered, picked, poked, bushed and gargled. Lathered with an intensity I hadn't seen before. He washed away every skerrick of dirt, in the process leaching all the natural oils and moisture from his skin before slathering himself with Nivea to return what soap had taken. It was a necessity, a ritual. As I watched him I wondered what he was trying to do away with. He did not smile or pleasure himself, he was not adding to or pampering himself, he was stripping away, eradicating, removing all trace. What, I speculated, could dirty a man so thoroughly and leave him so irritated by his own sweat, his own smell? What could leave him wanting to banish nature?

What was he trying to clean up?

Daniel had his no-go areas, the cordoned off parts of his world. The areas set with mines that I tip-toed about in, negotiating tripwires and small explosions. The big one I knew would either set us free or end us. It never came. After so many years together, though, I saw a picture of his family and what effect living with them, and then refusing them, had on him. A picture of a collection of people bound together in a neat suburban house holding their breaths under the slow leak of toxicity coming from his father. A toxic plume that settled over the family and ended with violent tirades, which his mother and siblings clamoured on top of each other to keep their heads above.

At night when I lay next to him, it was the smell of soap, above all else, that I held onto—above what else seeped out of him: the sleep talking, the night sweats, the-clutch-and-quick-release as I became a bit-player in a bad dream. It was the soap I breathed in. As I snuggled in close, it carried me away. The sweet musky scent reminding me of the little paper-covered soaps from the Flag-Inn motels we stayed at as kids, on the way to visit relatives in Melbourne. Soaps neatly placed on threadbare towels. Soaps bursting with floral scents, so different to the Solvol or Velvet soaps set by the bath at home, but still a smell of safety, of calm.

Pulling off the freeway and into the motel, Dad would ring the bell at reception. We would wait in the car while a robust, smiling woman in a house-dress ground his credit card through the machine, then handed him a key on a large block of wood with a number painted on it. We waited to be driven right up to the door of our room. The long shagpile carpet covering the floor of the clean room waited also, the small wooden nightstands next to the beds, a bible in one of the drawers, the controls for the radio and the nightlight in arms reach from the bed. Starched white sheets and heavy blankets folded hospital style, tough to kick out so you could cool your legs on a hot night in a close room. 'You must behave,' Mum would say with a sense of gravity, 'This is a motel, we're not in the middle of nowhere.' But we usually were. It was only the high, hot galvo fence around the whole place that lent it a sense of urbanity. It was only the fence that divided the motel with its pool, or an aged asphalt basketball court, from a huge dusty expanse of wheat stubble or the road into town.

At night. Dad snoring, Mum sleeping with one eye open, the sound of trucks on the freeway doing the late-night haul between Melbourne and Adelaide, the light from the neon sign tinting the thin, gauzy drapes with colour, the sound of the occupants in the next room, their muffled voices as they pottered about, sometimes a drunk lumbering from wall to wall, and the smell of the soap in the room.

In the morning. The car, wet with dew, waited just outside the door, the sleeping bags still rolled up tight in the back. Breakfast waiting on brown trays in the wooden breakfast box. Whitebread toast and vegemite, reconstituted orange juice, sweaty scrambled eggs under tin covers, cutlery in paper sheaths and sachets of salt and pepper. We ate breakfast watching TV, the regional news broadcast interrupted by ads for combine harvesters and boutiques. Dad pawing over the maps with toast in one hand, and a pen in the other, all lines seamlessly connecting to take us safely, stalwartly, to the next destination. Mum with a cigarette in one hand and a hairbrush in the other.

We'd leave the beds unmade, sheets and blankets kicked onto the floor. Left them for the maid to fix, just because we could. We were always only passing through on the way elsewhere, never to stay more than one night, the little bars of soap really only enough for one wash, two at the most. The paper wrapping in the bathroom bin that the maid would clean up too, leaving no trace we had ever cherished the cozy scene.

Witness

No. 7's a dead-shit. I hope he's out. On the tram on the way home I wasn't thinking about the old girl and I wasn't thinking about the small efforts she made, some lippy, patting her hair into shape, buttoning up her nightie. I wasn't thinking about Mandy sobbing up a storm, and I wasn't thinking about Daniel gone for good. I wasn't thinking about money and I wasn't thinking about sex. I wasn't thinking about the empty flat.

No. 7's a dead-shit. I hope he's out. Sometimes you need a witness, but this time I wanted to leave no trace. Because when there's no-one around to see how rancid you've become, then if it isn't seen, it didn't happen. You can sweep it under the rug and it's between you and the floor. You don't need anyone looking on and listening in and taking what's yours, because you'll never get any of it back and then it's done.

Uneasy identification

A hesitation of hopefuls, about five of them, in any number of disguises, watched. One of the men was so far undercover he stood out. This caused a man in a neat suit to eventually whisper when the others had dispersed and there was finally a loaded moment between them, 'Are you a cop?'

The white tiles, impossible to chip away at without the correct industrial tools, were still in good order. The mortar between the bricks, being damp and buttery, had, on the other hand, been gouged out with a pen, leaving a vent between the cubicles.

Dave

It was less lonely sitting and staring at whatever was or wasn't on the other side of the wall in the station toilets than it was to look through the gap between the partitions behind his computer. In the office he could peer undetected at Rebecca whenever she was at her desk, not doing her usual errands or standing up with her head over the partition talking. But time went nowhere. He could twiddle his pen and wonder about her hair and how dry it was, sometimes he traced the trimming around the neck of her t-shirt, sometimes he copied the pattern of her dress with his tongue on the roof of his mouth, twirling his tongue left then right near his teeth to imitate the big colourful swirls. As fascinating as it was to watch her, it made time go more slowly than if he actually did his work. Doing spreadsheets made lunch come around more quickly than not doing them.

The dialogue between them was as usual, zero. Not a word. Zip. Flinders Street Station had a reputation. Quick. Easy. Prone to bad hygiene. Sometimes dangerous. He was alert.

If the copper hadn't been purpose built for the job—buffed and butch and coming across as he was, inexperienced but obviously cruising for something—Dave might have used the urinal and moved on. He might never have looked sideways, and more than likely kept his hands to himself. Come to think of it, he wouldn't have used the urinal at all, but stayed in the cubicle like he usually did. Dave liked his privacy. He preferred to piss with a locked door behind him. He couldn't go easily with other men beside him and remembered being pushed against a wet urinal at school.

If the good-looking cop hadn't been in the building and undercover then the crime wouldn't have happened. This was his main gripe, what he came back to when the humiliation of it turned to anger. And if Dave had hooked up with someone in the cop's absence, then, without him there, it would've ceased to be a crime, no-one the wiser, with Dave back at his desk right on 1.30, a little less tense, a load off. It was entrapment.

Comfort

A terrible thought occurs to me: I cannot spend my life in a permanent state of orgasm. I am forced to dwell in the spaces on either side, anticipation or regret, fear or relief, life or loss.

I can wander parks, unshaven, wearing tracksuit pants and a Bonds t-shirt, my dick just that little bit harder than flaccid. I can duck into public toilets, read the messages on the cold walls, and stare indifferently at the other men, even, and sometimes especially, the ones I suck. I can flick through the pages of gay magazines, tantalised by the bronzed bodies, the stories, the personal ads, and the glossy catalogues catering for all tastes. I can sit for hours in front of the television, tamed by someone else's action in an X-rated video. I can cruise the bars, saunas, clubs, and swim centre, looking for others doing the same. I can call an ex-lover at 2am and get together in a warm familiar bed to act out an old scene. I can roam cyber-space or party hard on a phone chat-line. I may even meet you. And when all this leaves me wanting, I can work overtime and save hard for the latest home technologies in virtual reality and teledildonics.

I crave closeness at arm's length, intensities in short, startling bursts. I'm hopeful of the connections I make in everyday places, in everyday ways. I'm comforted knowing that somewhere out there guys are touching, entering taboo zones, spraying cum on everyday walls, men in suits, neat and tidy, men wearing hard hats and overalls, old Italian men with potbellies, mincing queens drowning in Versace aftershave, university students on pushbikes—they reassure me, affirm my desires, they turn me on. And even if I don't participate in these panting high jinks, I sleep more soundly knowing they happen.

Tony

At 6am Tony walked the dog like he was running late for a meeting. Really striding out. Going as fast as he could before breaking into a trot, or god forbid, a skip. After his sporting injury he no longer jogged, his body wasn't what it once was. It hadn't bounced back. He walked the dog like he was heading to the boardroom, and watch out because today heads were going to roll. Tony had slept rough. His tossing and turning broken only by the odd bad dream. He dreamed of Paula, that sinewy bitch he'd licked and fucked for ten long years before she finally took the kids and pissed off. He hated her. Stephanie was in there too. She was his current disappointment. And after only a few years it looked like if he didn't do something soon he'd end up in the same goddamn situation. Stephanie was driving him up the wall. He felt trapped. It was killing him. And here he was, sleeping with Stephanie and dreaming about Paula. What a disaster.

He worked his arse off too, fourteen hours a day, and for what? She didn't work, didn't clean, could barely cook, and any love that was there in the beginning had done what he should've done months ago, packed its bags and split. Any of what was once good between them had got

83

wise and shot through, not sticking around to endure their uncompromising existence, silence or screaming, and precious little between. And what remained when love left town was where he found himself now, confused and too scared to make another bad move.

Sure, he could move out, but it was his house and fuck it if that bitch was getting a penny of it. Had she earned it? No. On that he was clear. It had taken him nearly a decade to financially recover from Paula and he wasn't going to give Stephanie the same satisfaction. No way. He'd rather stew in the shit he'd created than have his success stolen from him. And he wasn't going to be seen as a failure, either. This was his second marriage, which, even though she'd been a goddamn nightmare to live with, he was conscious of the fact that it would be his second divorce. He didn't want the guys at the office or the golf club talking. He knew most of them couldn't give a damn about their own wives, and he wasn't going to be the one they used to deflect attention away from their own stinking home lives, making him the comparative case. He wasn't going to tell them and go through all of what it was like when he split from Paula, especially hearing those junior arse-licking pricks run Paula down when they drank at the pub. He hated that. He didn't like hearing it about Paula, and he wouldn't put up with it about Steph. A prime sow she might be, but he'd loved her once, or thought he had, and hadn't forgotten some of the good times between them. Probably, if the truth was told, he was really pretty sad that it hadn't worked out, that there just seemed no way to resolve the differences between them. For the moment though, she was still his wife, and if anyone was going to run her down it would be him. That much he knew for sure.

After his injury, walking at a good strong pace was what the chiropractor recommended. So that's what he did. He used the walking trails in the park around the Merri Creek. He drove his new Audi hatch to the park and walked from there. He walked to clear his head, to settle his anger at life's frustrations, and to keep his fifty-two year old body in shape. Tony was a handsome, silver-haired fox, with a well-preserved body. He intended to stay that way.

Doing warm-up stretches he noticed other men as they hung around the car park near the toilets. They wandered. They lurked. They sat in their cars with their heads turned down. They lent on the bonnets. They walked off into the thick scrub below the asphalt paths. He noticed.

Tony was one of the Kinsey Report's famous thirty-seven percent of men who'd had at least one homosexual experience in their youth. He'd had two. They happened in his second year of high school and he'd vowed they would never happen again.

People come to terms with their homosexuality at different rates. Some burst onto the scene, coming out with no signs and no warning. They detonate with complete disregard for who gets hurt in the process. Others just are, surprising no-one when they bring a partner of the same sex home to meet the family. 'Tell us something we don't already know.' Some never face their desires at all.

If Tony was ever going to blow, he had a very long fuse. He'd always done what was expected, taking into account the feelings of others and suppressing his own.

Over the years he'd been bothered very little by the prospect of sex with men. He thought about it occasionally and then pushed it out of his mind by submerging himself in work, fatherhood, being a worthy husband, kids every other weekend. Other than the breakdown with Paula and where he now found himself with Stephanie, he'd done a bloody good job. He was proud of what he'd achieved.

Queer things

Off the tram at Northcote High Street. Still sad from
seeing Mum was reason enough to take the long way
through the parks. Home would make me lonesome
crazy, set me pacing that ridiculously small room, working
up the threadbare rug and chaining the cigs.

It was our last move—into two huge buildings in the
harshest, bog-brown bricks you can imagine. It's
impossible to think they were ever in fashion—what a
dank and spiteful colour in an otherwise pretty
neighbourhood. The apartment blocks sit like two parallel
turds. Brown logs side by side. Lovelorn, the windows of
one block stare into the eyes of the other, perpetually
gazing into their own abject disappointment.

When we moved in no-one said welcome or came out.
But you could feel them. When I dropped my end of the
couch getting it up the stairs and Daniel went quick to the
end of his tether and then let his end go, you could feel
them then. And still no-one came to lend a hand—not
No. 7, who saw it all, not No. 9. But we took the plants
left behind in the flat as a gift and once Dan Jiffed the
whole place down, we set about making a home, with the
gardenia by the door.

Recently, a returned war veteran who lived at No. 5, and whose late-night turns rivalled his smell as a good enough reason to stay away, shot himself. It was the most public event to happen in the block since the kid from No. 10 went berserk and ran into an oncoming car. Everybody turned out. The detectives door knocked, questioning the occupants of the flats, who of course had heard nothing, but used the shot to the head as a chance to whinge about what a noisy prick No. 5 had been.

I headed down Westgarth Street towards the bike tracks near the creek. It was four o'clock and the traffic had begun its loud hum. People were in the park, jogging, walking dogs, kicking footballs. I crossed Heidelberg Road and cut through the scrub. I walked by the creek, even though the council had cut back all the privacy and made the whole bank nothing but stumps and rivulets of mud. Rain had not only washed the freshly disturbed soil from the upside of the riverbank down towards its inevitable destination, dragging it into the fast-running torrent, but had also flushed rubbish downstream in a violent purge.

Chip packets, waxy milk cartons, pieces of cardboard, long stringy bits of unidentifiable industrial offal, and most obviously, masses of white plastic shopping bags gripped the dead sticks which had jammed along the riverbanks as you'd expect after such a spate. The shopping bags flapped in the wind like white flags waving against the mess of war.

It used to be that cruising happened all along the bank, way up to the barbecue hut, then up the slope to the toilets. The creek bank was a maze of carved out nooks and semi-protected crannies. Air pockets of scrub connected by well-trodden tracks, lines of desire, lines of flight. You held your breath. You could walk into one pod and have your fantasies come true with a guy who wouldn't hold you to ransom or expect any more from you than he himself could give. He wouldn't want any more than what the two of you could create there in the scrub. Usually just sex. Perfunctory. A distraction. Which is always so much more. Moments that rub against loneliness and betrayal, smoothing out their edges that you catch yourself on throughout the day. Sometimes more than you expect: calling out and finding an answer where only silence and agitation had been minutes before. Usually just sex, I told myself. A release. Other times though, a bit of a talk after. Maybe a made-up name, one time Andrew, another time Nigel. Sometimes, 'By the way, my name is Lennie' and out with the truth, about all sorts. Sometimes a real warm feeling and a laugh. An embarrassed laugh as you used the hankie. 'You're cute, when are you here next?' A touch on the elbow, a pat on the back, a wink. 'You ever seen the cops around, mate? Make sure you take care.' And a walk back to the cars together.

I loved it.

At other times the chambers would be empty and you'd simply be confronted with your own stupidity at ever thinking you'd find escape or solace. That you'd find passion to go on with.

I hated it.

Head down and kicking at small clumps of mud baking in the late afternoon sun, I remembered the times I'd had success and the times I'd walked home alone. I kicked at the half-hardened furrows, careful to discern the occasional stack of shit left by a defiant or lazy dog owner. I felt okay. I was beginning to settle. Mum had been in before and she'd come out before. She'd juggled her medication, she'd gone along fine for a bit; something had happened, she'd freaked out and gone back to hospital. Lithium, Prozac, Luvox, Zoloft. Grief, hatred, anger, sadness turned inwards. A relapse. I'd seen it before. She was chasing her tail. She knew it. I knew it. The doctors knew it. The drug companies depended on it. But so far she had survived. For years. 'March winds and April showers bring forth May flowers' was what she used to say when she was going under.

To her children. 'All will be fine,' she sometimes said too when the nurses led her up the corridors and away.

The scrub and trees were mostly cleared—the aim being to encourage native wildlife to return to the willow-choked water, or so I read in *The Leader*. But there was little point now cruising the banks with joggers and cyclists looking down, saddened that their dirty little tell-all Sunday sideshow had been given its marching orders. What I reckon: cutting down the trees and shaving life from this place was the way the council got to say, 'Pull Your Pants Up And Get The Hell Outta Here With Your Sick Arse Way Of Behaving', without actually saying it. Really, could they put up a sign showing two guys going at it from behind in the park, with a red circle and red line through them, placed next to the Dispose of Garbage Correctly sign?

No. So instead, the more polite option was hit upon and in came the trucks and chainsaws and a gang of meaty workers. Workers making sure there was more room to move and less chance of stumbling across something they'd have to go looking for to find anyway.

I walked along the exposed riverbank, still using the old trails that once cut through the willows. Old condom wrappers and lube packets had resisted the clean-up and memorialised past connections. I headed to the barbecue hut to sit down and rest and watch the comings and goings from the bog. The red Commodore was parked in its usual spot and the blue van was there for an early dinner. A hotted-up Mazda was making a cameo, and an expensive European hatch was doing an anxious drive-by. Car bodies stood in for the pulsating masses of horny gristle that drove them, which, in turn, became the hearts of the machines. Cars idled: a language of desire beckoned and repelled, incorrigible, offhand, unpredictable. A brakelight winked, a U-turn screamed, 'Oy, this way boy', and a cluster of cars in an otherwise open space was as exclusive as an orgy already underway, snobbing you off.

I watched from a park bench as people made their way to the toilets. I wouldn't let myself take part in whatever was going on behind the brick walls. Not now. Not yet. I simply watched, calmed by other people's defiance. I watched their public displays of pleasure as they walked in and out of the toilet, as they drove back and forth in their cars. They flirted with the world around them regardless of who looked on. No pretense made for being in the park for any other reason than their own recreation. They held their heads high and stuck to their guns as though it was no more a crime than two brothers kicking a football, a father turning a sausage on the sizzle,-or a mother removing the cling-wrap from a fly-away sponge.

Later I'd unglue myself from the slats of the park bench—all three of which had graffiti scribbled across them:

DO YOU CONFORM TO HETEROSEXUALITY BECAUSE IT'S EASY?

HAVE YOU EVER SERIOUSLY CONSIDERED YOUR SEXUALITY?

ARE YOU HETEROSEXUAL BY DEFAULT?

The graffiti unsettled me. It put in writing a homosexual presence that I wanted to go unnoticed. It made the presence visible, my presence visible. It put it out there. It put me out there. A small story inscribed on a park bench that wouldn't let me alone. I felt embarrassed when I read the lines: a hot flush for the pervy man who has no life, and who we can all see. You. You. You. The man in white shoes who thinks he passes and gets away. You.

I uncrossed my legs and kept my feet wide apart on the concrete. Flat. Anything that might be construed as feminine or queeny stripped from my facade, I hoped. I forced myself to make contact with anyone in the park who didn't give me the furtive glance of a fag. I forced myself to smile and look at their eyes. A weak smile. Feigned camaraderie trapped me between two worlds. I wanted them to believe something about me that I didn't believe myself. That I was okay. That I was good. That I belonged to these people who I watched going about their lives in straightforward and uncompromised ways. But I didn't belong. I hated them. Hated the way I propped up their world of respectability, refusing to come out. I prolonged my longing and forced my debasement, my desire, to wait.

You know nothing of me. Fuck you. Fuck your kids in pushers. Fuck your dogs. Fuck you in the sunshine. And fuck how the sun bounces off your clean car. Fuck your push-ups, your fit legs, your running shoes. You know nothing of me. I'm not a fag. I'm not a hetero. I'm not the paedophile you've read about in the papers. I'm not your brother, your husband, your son. I'm not happy. I'm not sad. I'm not smiling. I'm not meditating. I'm not relaxing. I'm not waiting for a friend. I'm not part of an absent crowd. I'm not alone. I'm not here for anything you can imagine. I'm not here at all.

Angry and sad and resigned and needing to piss. But the public toilet was somehow out of bounds for this simple need and mocked me. I felt unwelcome, even fraudulent at needing to use it to piss. I wasn't part of what was going on in there. Did I belong anywhere?

I touched his shoulder. I pulled away without contempt in the hospital toilet. 'You are my last hope for this moment,' was what I saw in his face, his plastic Ken-doll face from which products and exfoliants had peeled layers of life, making him look, more than anything, translucent. 'Don't make me live this moment alone. I will fall and break right here on the tiles. Take this moment in your hand and throw it away, in your mouth and suck at it, swallow it. Make my suspicion of the receptionist on the desk worth it. Make the risk I took worth it. Show me one more time that I survived. Show me I made it out alive. Make me a worthwhile moment.' That's what I saw in the seconds when I said, 'Let's leave it, mate,' and zipped up, touched his shoulder gently, and walked out.

The guy from the red Commodore walked towards the toilet and glanced my way. Two other men had gone in a while back and still hadn't come out. I waited, a tightness in my bladder. Sometimes men parked their cars, got out fast and jogged to the toilet with a look of urgency in their faces. Needing a piss became a mock performance to justify a quick stop to blow their brains out at a public toilet in the middle of a busy workday. It was usually men in suits, men with nice cars. Men kidding themselves they had more to lose if they were detected. More face to save. They jogged or quickly walked to the toilet. Head down, needing to pee. It was a lame ruse.

I preferred men who'd given up on the performance and just hung around. I preferred them to loiter and play the game. I preferred men who cruised. Jeans, sneakers, a t-shirt, an afternoon given up. Time on their hands.

I watched from the park bench. People with the legitimate business of leisure or exercise or walking dogs were staking their claims on the park, but I was unwilling to fight for the democracy of space. It had been carved up and I'd been left out. Who cared?

A woman pulled a poop bag from the dispenser near the fence. A silver-haired man laced up his shoes in preparation for a jog. While stretching his leg muscles he gave the men walking into the toilet an occasional uncommitted stare. A couple with a basket and rug headed for the sloping knoll with the city views. It seemed ridiculous to expect they didn't know or didn't care about the sexy vibe in the air around them when she did the pointing, going, 'Here, here,' and he flung out the rug. I watched them glance up each time someone went into the dunnies, her with the baguette and the cheese, him with the corkscrew and the bottle, both forgetting to notice the city view and changing colour of the sky after 5. Unsaid between them, but you could tell. Of course they knew. Perhaps in their own way they'd parked their picnic rug in view of the toilet block to soak up the intoxicants that swirled around it like pollen. Perhaps they'd use them to mark their own desires and the unbridled fucking they'd later do. Tonight in the bedroom they'd fuck like wild, more wildly than they had in ages. I bet you. What they could only imagine was going on in the toilets would make its virile presence felt. And to them it was unimaginable that such a sleazy sexual surrogate could intrude on their lives, sliming its way into their bed. Yet tonight after their picnic in the park and their voyeuristic fascination for the men cruising around them, it would just so happen that they would both feel a little bit more alive, a wee bit more potent. Tonight they would *fuck*. It was a queer thing.

I watched on, no need to move, no need to get involved. No need to become pleasure for them. I wasn't there for what they imagined. I wasn't there at all.

Splowing

When I met Mandy outside the club she was blowing out smoke. Alpine Lights and loving it.

Inside, the barman saw us and by the time he said, 'The usual?' and Mandy went, 'As Puuurrr,'—all sexy and eyelashes and a tip of the shoulder—he already had two spirit glasses in his hand and was turning away giving each a shot of vodka from the dispenser on the wall.

All Bound For Moo Moo Land was playing on the jukebox. Retro heaven. When we heard it, we both said 'Inspired' at the same time. We said it long and slow but with an up tone, 'In-sp-ir-ed'. We said it about what we loved. It was our word. And we loved that song. Trust The KLF to haul Tammy out of the wastelands and back to the clubs—some tips, some back-combing, a new hairdo and a new song—Wow, go Tammy go.

Mandy had been working at the hairdresser's, herself fluffing, blowing and back-combing. All day long going hell for leather with the foils, touching up the roots and doing the odd blue rinse. Perms a rarity.

She took a sip of vodka then dragged on a ciggy.

'I've been held captive for far too long, hair products are peeving me. I can't find the right one.'

'What's the problem?'

'They shit me to tears.'

She poked at her hair.

'String, look at it. Straw. You'd think me, with all the products and potions in the world at my disposal would be able to settle for one that works and can keep me happy. There must be one out there that's right. There has to be!'

She rattled off a list of the products she'd tried, in an over-it but rapid-fire way. She recited the list with a real give-a-shit tone.

'Shane, Mark, Schitzo Benny, Pin Ed, Michael, I know what you mean,' I said. 'We're sluts for the next best thing, but really we just want to settle down. What we need is a break from all this bloody choice. We need to get real about what's important. Grab one by the nuts and hang on. Don't let go. That's what I used to think, anyway. Keep him at all costs. Now … Now I don't know.'

'Splowing,' she said, 'that's the latest.'

'Yeah?' I went, lifting my eyebrow.

'It's the latest trick from New York. Apparently, god-forbid, big hair is making a comeback. It's a combination of hair spraying and blow-drying.'

'Go on.'

'You tease the shit out of the hair, then, in a quick-draw way, cocking both pistols, you let rip with the hairdryer and the spray can at the same time, spraying and blowing—Splowing.'

'Crikey,' I said. 'What does it look like?'

'Big, absolutely Big.'

'I'll have to try that the next time I've got trade, blow and spray 'em at the same time—Hey Baby, how about a splow-job.'

'You're all right though,' she said, mussing the bristles on my three-day growth. 'No hair, no problems. I never thought I'd see you looking like a tennis ball. And single.'

Mandy was warm. She always showed how much she liked me. She moved her hand from my head down to my face, touching my cheek as she took her hand away.

'It's been a while he's not around. I'm surprised,' she continued, 'I thought you'd pull out all the stops and go after him. You love your relationships, your one-on-ones.'

She was right in a way. When I'd first come out, I'd found someone to justify my declaration. And I was loyal, more or less, for a long time. For much of my life I'd been someone's other half.

'I hate it. I just can't stand no-one to talk to in the mornings. I've always hated it: the quiet of the morning. To shave in a silent house, to apply deodorant and have no-one complain about the fumes; it's a nightmare. Morning radio, the sound of upstairs flushing, a beeping alarm from next-door, people screwing: how depressing. They're noises made by someone else, but they're not life.'

The barman kept an eye on us, monitoring our glasses, as a good barman does. I gave him a nod and again he turned to the dispenser on the wall. Mandy looked at him, at me, as I talked.

'I want to sort the mail of two people. I want a calendar on the wall with filled-in squares. I want to double-book then have to cancel.

'Thirteen, eighteen, twenty-two years, you spend all that time, you know, rehearsing the day when you'll come out, when you choose to finally fucking-well say, This Is Me. I'm not like you! I'm not like you. And for what? To end up eating alone in front of the telly; to flick through futile magazines; to be online searching to fill the other side of the bed. To have someone. That deadshit from the flats who shot himself? He wasn't found for days, and when he was—you know what I heard?—it was blokes from the pub who had to scrape his head off the ceiling and clean up for the landlord. And when he was gone the thing I noticed, his telly was finally off.'

Anything's possible

Okay boys. Remember the days when you still had those intense, unsettling wet dreams? Remember waking up with a wet patch on the front of your PJ bottoms and being alarmed and excited at the same time? Now they seem almost quaint—out of style—but remember the intensity of feelings, the buzz, the bodies, the explosion, and the fireworks. Remember trying to find the real world again after such a wild ride, which you did in the darkness by detecting a beacon and working from there, a wardrobe, another sleeping body in the room, the streetlight outside the window, anything to help put you back together, one spellbound piece at a time? Remember waking up and being alone again in bed?

Remember surprising Mum by doing your own laundry, for a day—wanting to be as discreet as possible but still having to ask how much powder to use and how to turn the machine on. Remember that? Remember when the preamble part of the dream cut to the pre-cum phase and you transformed into a Russian gymnast (or was it a yoga master), it doesn't matter, the point is, in your dreams your body had a remarkable plasticity and you were so bloody experimental, anything was possible. Remember?

Show me more nameless faces

'Here,' he said, thrusting the small bottle towards me.

'No thanks,' I said.

That was it. Nothing more. I could've gone on to say more and I did want to compliment him for something, but under the circumstances, I couldn't think what. Just saying 'no thanks' really didn't seem enough considering he was approaching the whole incident like an opening night gala. He seemed so bloody proud of what he'd obviously practised long and hard at, and what was now getting an overdue public viewing. It just didn't measure up to say only 'no thanks' with virtually no eye contact as I stood back and watched the whole frou-frou show unfold. It didn't measure up at all.

As much as it's possible in a cubicle, he was strutting his stuff, shaking his girdled box, doing a turn for whoever cared to watch from the stalls. The thrill and blatant disregard of someone in the grip of naughtiness was obvious. With the door open—first just ajar and then slowly pulled back—there he was with his tights in lights. Totally out there. Sheer exhibitionism.

He was wearing green lace panties and at first it frightened me. I was startled. It was a luxury I tried hard to repel. At first I wanted to flee, but after the initial shock and embarrassment, I couldn't take my eyes away. I was riveted. I stayed to see what would happen next.

Lace, even cheap looking lace—harsh lace—can pull you in. It looks invitingly smooth next to the bristly, hairy legs and hairy guts of a middle-aged man. I wanted to reach out and touch it. Stroke it. Just to see.

It surprised me because this was a man's man type of guy, older, with a tough edge, straight acting. He was no pussycat. His cracked, furrowed face seemed painted in thick broad strokes with a stiff brush, and then stippled with a thick coating of freckles and sunspots. His ginger moustache and eyebrows were unkempt. Brown canvas over-alls gathered in a heap around his ankles, lending him the appearance of a tall slender bush planted in a mound of compost. It surprised me to see him in knickers, and it surprised me to see there was another guy in the cubicle too who didn't look the least bit worried. Other than me having walked in and given them both a moment's startle so that they jumped back as though they both, in various states of undress, hadn't really even noticed each other there at all.

The scene was one of happy enthusiasm, a careless moment of fun, but still I felt bad watching. Mostly I felt bad for me, but I felt a bit bad for him as well. Being there in green lace panties in a stinking cubicle is embarrassing, and I wondered as I walked back to the bench what his life was like on either side of what he was now doing. Who was he after he pulled at the gapping sides of his overalls, drawing them closed like theatre curtains, and stepped out into the world? Who was he with his lace concealed?

He shakily replaced the cap of the bottle he'd sniffed at, waited a few seconds for the rush, and then, you could just tell, was whacked by it. He closed his eyes, melted back into the wall he was leaning on, and let the man in front of him, a handsome wog boy, suck him. The lacy veil covering his penis turned back by the dutiful groom who, on his knees, consummated the event with a kiss. With voyeuristic fascination I looked on. I did not move. Lead-footed. Beating heart. A rush.

Joe

His father's fury was laced with spittle. When he yelled,
'Joe, a fag?' in English, you could have wiped it off the
wall. For Joe it was a sad triumph: he was out.

Tony

At 7pm Tony secured the laces of his runners with a double knot. He walked across the car park to the toilet, aware of a man who'd wandered in when he'd begun his stretches and still hadn't come out. At the urinal Tony peed and listened. No noise from the cubicle. The door shut but not locked. Someone behind it. Tony found this a bit odd. He washed his hands as a pretext to stay in the toilet block longer, all the while keeping his eyes on the door. All his attention moved to the lock's vacant sign on the door's closed panel with its green letters. Curiosity and fear worked at him, entwining themselves around his muscular, hairy legs and holding him in the stinking unfamiliar environment. The brown bricks of the walls were rough and hard. He thought about being grated on them and winced in his gut, imagining the torn skin, deep cuts, and blood. A flash thought.

Back at school it happened twice and both times he felt how he was feeling now. He was tense with a curiosity that kept him from walking away, and gave his body an allover uneasy feeling like cockroaches doing the jitter-bug under his skin, shaking their dandy arses. The back of his neck was hot. His groin was alive—fight or flight mechanisms kicked in. He felt like he might crap.

At the end of 1966 Australians were mourning the death of Harold Holt, some still holding their breath for when he'd walk out of the sea like a son returned. Tony was holding his breath that Randal would keep his mouth shut about sucking him off down the back of the oval at lunchtime. He was a fool to be seduced once, and a fucking idiot returning for a second go. If the truth was told, he could barely remember the blurred details of the sin that took place. He could barely remember why he'd even made friends with Randal that week and why they'd ended up under the canopy of the old pine tree on a day when the rest of the class was berserk anticipating the summer break. How it happened Tony couldn't quite say, but it haunted him that summer until it became clear Randal knew what was good for him.

Randal was the school pansy. Through lack of resistance and astonishing fortitude he had found a kind of freedom in the role. He walked with a transcendent air, insults and assassinations of character seeming to slide off the Vaselined veneer he was forced to create. Homo, horse's hoof, cream puff, ginger beer, queer, queen, ponce, precious, pansy, fairy, fancy pants, tonk. It was a chorus that followed him around the schoolyard and sometimes through the streets as he walked home, a choir in the lower registers.

It was rumoured Randal could be found in the toilets at lunchtime playing with other boys, although he was never there on the days a posse formed to find out for sure. Proof or no proof, there was no doubt about the status of boys like Randal. Tony wanted nothing to do

106

with what the gang might find; he wanted no reminders. He stopped following the posse to the toilets and he never let on about the meeting under the pine canopy behind the oval. For forty years a secret.

The door opened slowly from the inside. The more Tony looked the wider it opened and the more was revealed. Hair long and greasy, pants around his calves, penis standing out hard, the foreskin receding from the knob at the end. It looked like the handbrake of the Audi after Tony pulled on it to secure his most precious possession. It stood up at the same forty-five degree angle.

The two men stared at each other in a fiery flash. When Tony held his ground, The Handbrake started immediately to slowly pull his closed fist back and forth, slowly massaging himself. Leaning back against the cistern, he stretched his legs forward and lifted his jumper to accentuate his exposure. Tony's black Labrador rolling on its back and wagging its tail when he returned from work couldn't have been more vulnerable, more open. The man was smug and sleazy and relaxed.

Tony was basically gone the moment he stepped into the cubicle. And the moment he did, The Handbrake sat bolt upright, grabbed at Tony's running shorts with one hand—immediately exposing his penis through the leg hole—and pulled him forward from behind with the other hand. Tony reeled back in his head and steadied himself with the architrave of the cubicle door. Under the sway of the groping arm his feet shuffled forward, causing the architrave—his anchor to the real world of what he knew and what he counted on—to slip from his fingers. His arms went up from the sides of his body in the way they did when Mrs. Doyle came at him to take measurements for his school pants at the haberdashery. He was awkward and lanky then; he was no better now. His body not his own, pulled at the hips, unbalanced at the feet, flushed in the face, sweaty under the arms, handled like a mid-priced cut of meat. For The Handbrake it wasn't new and it wasn't special. It was simply the next.

Tony's body not his own. The Handbrake had been where Tony was falling a thousand times before. Tony fell. Deep. Deep. Deeper. No longer himself. No longer the walls of the cubicle, no longer the urinal or the sink, no longer the car outside or the walking tracks. No longer house or home, no children, no office, no office politics, no secretary, no accounts payable. No longer the CPA annual dinner, no longer the annual address, and no longer a speech to write. No longer the lawns or the lawnmower. No longer himself, and no time to change his mind. No time at all. Gone.

The warm velvety lining of a man's mouth. The urgent, quick, unashamed way he was being devoured. Desire at full bore. Unrestrained need. Where had he been to have missed all this? Paula, Stephanie, what had it been with them, obligation, guilt, a sleazy transaction? He could feel the hesitation and duty in the times they'd given him oral sex. Their tentative lips and shallow gags let him know the pleasure was for him and not for them. His heavy hand behind their heads, always edging them a little further forward, guiding them down, wishing them to be willing and ferocious. So restrained.

The head bobbed in front of him. Thrashed and gobbled. The hair parted sharp down the middle. The part like the white strip down an asphalt road. Specks of dandruff splattered like roadkill along the strip, white domestic animals hit by something they never saw coming. Never saw coming at all.

A phone number above the cistern in black Texta. The numbers partied, blurred, agitated and smudged. Over it, perhaps, from the long wait. Water marks swirled on the stained white plasterboard running between the ceiling and the harsh brick. *Tony's daughter radiant in aqua watermarked taffeta at a recent wedding. Tony an upstanding member of the community. Tony looking down.* The head bobbed. *Tony falling down.*

His married legs were pried apart. *Backdoor bandit, bronzer, fag, fairy, freckle-puncher, fruit, mattress-muncher, pillow-biter, poofter, poo-jabber, shirt-lifter, shit-stabber, doughnut puncher, the Hole of Calcutta.* Just far enough for The Handbrake to finger a little further through a part of Tony's life he thought he had kept well-closed.

Wait. What? Stop. What are you doing? He's putting a finger in me. I had a shit before I left to go walking. No. Am I clean? Stop. My legs are shaking. Is the door locked? Police. Children. Anybody out there? Stop. Pull out. Pull away. Turn and Run. I will come. Inside your mouth. Stop. Wait.

The Handbrake didn't stop anything. He kept at Tony. One hand up the back of his running shorts and his face to the front of them. Adidas silk at his cheek. The elastic band still tight around Tony's waist. And the green letters still saying vacant. Tony was slipping. Tony not Tony. Tony dragged from his moorings.

Not shedding tears

Standing in a backroom of scrub at the side of the freeway, I smoked two Stuyvys in quick succession. Zipped up high to the throat. Beanie down. 'Cold is the night when the stars shine bright,' Mum used to say. From the outside, the scrub seemed impenetrable. A dark opaque mass bought into relief by the floodlights around the oval nearby. Now that I was on the inside looking out, the density had broken down. I could make out the water of the creek and a small cluster of newly planted trees, some of which had been battered by the rain and wind and were lying down in the grass. I could make out the way the grass on the vast hill had been mown in long parallel sweeps, leaving it to dry like neat cornrows of blond hair. I could see cars driving into the car park, and beyond to the bridge over the freeway and the access roads. It's the reverse of how you can see into a lit window at night from the outside, but not see outside once you're in.

He approached me the way you'd approach any prized possession prone to flight. But I wasn't going anywhere. And I needed to feel sorry for someone so he'd do. He moved out of the shadows. Face peculiar and ugly. He circled me gingerly, making no sudden moves.

Backlighting thrown from the freeway gave him a ghastly glow, and I looked away. In another time he might have occupied the celluloid of some perverse Hollywood film. Beady eyes and pixie ears, a button nose and mean floating mouth on that fat face would be his calling card, and him sucking cock with those Dental Floss thin lips—clamped on like it was his last chance to shine—his signature move. The audience transfixed by abjection. I held my ground. Planted my feet. He would do.

He sized me up, speculatively assessing the risk before taking it. Then touched me like I was a bubble or a mysterious unknown substance, or a vapour, something ethereal you really can't grasp. With one hand I pushed down on his shoulder, with the other I pulled myself. The invitation exhausted any resistance his body had and he plummeted like a mango rolling off a table (careful mate, you'll kneecap yourself). On getting the go-ahead, any concern about me doing a magic disappearing trick was turned into an expectation that soon enough I would, and he'd again be alone. He started making the most of the time he had. He expected rejection. He knew why he was on his knees and why I wasn't. In the same way that a cumbersome fire-truck loaded with men and hoses and water works up speed in the direction of a disaster, he lumbered towards the urgency of his orgasm. Filled with contempt and loathing, for him, for me, for the situation, I looked down on his thinning hair. My eyes adjusted to the darkness and I saw more clearly the generosity of my gesture. I'd stroke him, but it was all I could do to touch him as I grabbed the back of his head and pushed it further into my groin. I felt bad.

I needed to go to the limit and considered stroking his hair. I considered touching it tenderly like a mother sweeping her fingers across the forehead of a child and curling its sun-kissed fringe behind its darling little ear— I'd like to have that much love. To give. To care. But I didn't. He made me want to puke. I'm generous, but no bloody Saint.

I didn't draw away from the places of disgust I tracked down on his body; I needed to feel sorry for someone. I sought them out; I magnified them. My compass, tending south, flicked occasionally towards true north, stiffened by the pallor of his aging tones, the blotches on the skin of the hands that touched at me, the shape of the ears I looked down on. I knew if I stayed with him long enough I would find pleasure, not in spite of these blemishes but because of them. I sought them out for relief.

My senses were alert as I contended with the dim reasons I invent to justify my longing: why him with the bad smell, the smudged glasses, with those hands. I had to face the fact I wanted to be there and had chosen this man, this moment, above all others. I'd found a difference that was almost intolerable, but was compelled to finish what I'd begun. Turn. Pull out. Walk away. But I couldn't escape the part of me that had been shaved off from respectability and was nourished in the moment. Hope makes use of weird traps. I spread my legs a little to steady myself. He looked up at me as though I was a hungry camera lens and this was a scene from any number of repetitious porno films. His eyes—not Jeff Striker, Joey Stefano, or the Bel Ami boys. Not the kings of porn. But the men who never made it more than once in West Hollywood. In low-grade studios. Men with red eyes and pimply arses being slam fucked on floodlit sets. Trying to look like they're enjoying it, getting off, having a blast. He looked up at me expectantly, sadly, humiliated, wanting, like a child. All in the eyes. I looked down on him. WHAT? WHAT? I looked down on him and reigned over his world that I knew nothing about. To me he was simply the well-kept Ford sedan neatly reversed into its usual spot near the pine palings. A nothing, nobody. We barely connected before he looked away. A cursory glance, a glimpse my way. He peeked up, looking at me for as long as he could, which really was only a few seconds. When our eyes met it was like looking into a mirror. Our retinas would be burned out if we held this gaze for too long, marvelling in the embarrassment of being face to face, of noticing we had found each other. So we didn't. Even at the height of desperation I tried to conceal myself and looked away.

My indifference didn't bother me. Why should it? We both knew why we were there, and that soon we would evacuate the space and move on, not having to commit ourselves to the moment or think about it later, unless we wanted to. Some sex is really only the equivalent of getting a hefty slap in the face. It's startling. It gets your attention. For a few brief seconds it saves you, perhaps. It shows you how alive you can be by bringing you back from the deadlands where you usually spin. Afterwards though, you have to blink to regain your orientation, and when you notice the other person you turn your back. You don't even pretend to care. You don't wait for him to come. It's no longer your concern. The smack of bodies is too much to bear and you're stripped too far back, completely undressed. You leave the scene. Suddenly, with your pants a long way down at your boots and your white arse hanging out, you feel overwhelmingly embarrassed, a stupid fool, a pervert, a depraved nitwit, and you don't need anyone there to confirm it. The whole hopeful episode as dangerous and ill-advised as running with scissors, but you did it anyway.

Two more thrusts and I blew. The stranger swallowed. He ingested the despair and contempt I was unconcerned about passing on. Tears left unshed turn to poison and are excreted from the body, transmitted from one person to another in a show of frantic fucking: fluids that joined us, for a moment, in a shrouded community of strangers.

Pre-cum used to be called *distillate of love*; doesn't that sound like tears to you? Unshed sadness stops men protecting themselves from risk and sends some chasing the devouring bug: sadness transferred between them as they dance their quickstep of hostile glances.

The stranger swallowed and walked away from me without a word. His dry eyes watched his feet tracing the path to the car park.

Without fuss he left. I did not mind. I'd taken what I could, and I was done. I lit a Stuyvy. Smoke fucked the night mist and was gone. I immediately started trailing a rough-looking bloke I'd passed earlier. I needed other men, one, two, three, maybe—maybe more. Then when I was drained, when the poison was leeched from me, when I was finally sucked dry, and the clouds had put the stars to bed, I would go home, to the flat, to sleep.

A fragment of a dream

Black smoke is billowing from somewhere near the emergency exit and the flight attendants have long ceased to be of any real use. The blonde with long red nails, tight hair, and clumps of gold on her wrists and fingers, is slapping a colleague in the face. He's gone to pieces. There is no obvious explanation for why the plane is entering a downward spiral: a mechanical fault, terrorism, an act of God? There are only a few bumps now. Oddly enough, the drinks trolley is disrupted to the point of a neat jiggle, nothing worse. People are fumbling for life jackets. The more functional attendants are trying to keep people seated, urging them to put their heads between their knees and assume the crash position. Through the mayhem I hear a woman speaking in a soothing voice to a child in the row behind. 'Someone will fix the problem, it's alright, sweetheart, it's just a small problem,' she's saying, the cracks in her voice going against what comes out of her mouth. For the first time in my life I surprise myself with calmness. I'm overcome with a deep sense of trust—what will be will be. I take the hand of the woman sitting next to me. We both know we're travelling on a doomed flight. Her hand is cold with sweat and trembling gently. People around us have lost the plot. Every emotion in the book is on display as I squeeze this woman's hand and tell her that everything will be fine. I tell her that I love her, love humanity, that the world is a benign place. It's a very real moment and I'm certain she won't reject me, not even if she wants to.

The dutiful son stops listening

The cold wind gave my face a good hard slap, but it wasn't enough to bring me around. Thoughts coagulated, one jamming up against another so there was no clean line, no clear direction. Nostalgic ruminations trailed off with no resolution. The loose ends found each other and tangled into a knot in my gut. I walked towards the park bench, which faithfully waited, steadfast as an old friend. Daniel was one of the loose ends. A badgering loose end. Just Daniel—at breakfast, lunch and tea. Him and me in bed, him and me in the street, him and me at the movies, at Safeway, on a tram holding hands. Me at twenty-four and ready to love, him wiping the town clean with his smug catch. 'A fresh start,' he said, and we were a couple, an us. Us in bed late, us at a dance party, us through a glory hole in a sex club wall. Me at twenty-five and on my knees looking for missing money. The first time. Him out of it, on the nod, barely saying, 'As if,' with his roll-down-shutter eyes, and me learning the long, hard, slow way not to trust, but to bargain. Me trying the tough love. Me at twenty-seven and loved down to the stumps, thin, but still up for it: a good cuddle, a good fight. Me turning twenty-eight. Daniel with flowers in his rough-as-you-like hands, the card yelling I love you, in capitals. Him still smelling like he did when I was twenty-four, still fingers smelling of smoke, still a warm comfort, still my fella. Suddenly me at twenty-nine.

The grass edging the path sent out runners onto the bitumen, a slow uniform march to claim back the space stolen by the grey tar. If I had my Walkman with me, I'd turn it up loud, play something hard, something smashing. I'd drown out the babbling past that I wear like a hairshirt to irritate my sense of being a letdown. I have the choice to walk here now and to sit on the bench or wait in the quiet space of a toilet cubicle. I make the choice to walk towards a deep pool of sadness rather than away from it. I am a penitent and this is what I must do. I head towards the cubicle. I convince myself that if I ache enough, I might, in the end, be granted relief. I take endless risks based on this hope.

And I've been here before, with all I can possibly give without breaking not being enough—a sick Granny leaning forward on her deathbed when I was a kid, the dog being hit by a speeding car and the vet saying that nothing could be done, no amount of stroking would bring him back. A primary school teacher with caked-on lip gloss and budgie-blue eye shadow telling me not to lie and me refusing to admit I stole some feeble piece of stationery from the classroom cupboard, digging my heels in until the recess bell broke me and I started to cry, giving her what she wanted. Lingering over the decision between the brown or blue Levi cords in the junior boys' section of a department store and then being rushed into the wrong colour, giving Mum what she wanted me to have, how she wanted me to look, her precious boy. Another report card saying could try harder. Sneaking into the bathroom to shave for the first time with a half-blunt LadyShave disposable, no celebration, only shame. Being the first boy in class to have hair under his arms, telling the popular blonde girl I loved her and seeing a foreskin on the same day. Kissing a girl because I'd been told I wanted to, turning away from a boy my own age because I'd been told I wasn't allowed to; in silent desperation turning to a man three times my age. Being fifteen and riding out a sexually transmitted infection, no information, no support, the weeping sore stinging late into the night. Back then you didn't ask questions, you were left to figure things out on your own. You tossed a problem around in your head. Twisted and turned it like a Rubik's cube, the broad simple strokes of primary emotions mixed into a frantic, irreversible palette of doubt and confusion. In those days it was stacked against you. You didn't ask questions, and you didn't answer back.

I bypassed the bench and headed straight for the toilets. The cubicles were disgusting. I pushed the first door back and saw the cold steel bowl choking with shit and toilet paper. Partially disintegrated turds visible in the brown water licked at the bowl's metal rim. The shit that must be flushed away for life to flourish floated before me in the blocked cesspool. My eyes ricocheted away from it. The foul sight revolted me but there was no corresponding smell, nothing localised as the whole chamber shut in its own skunk-like repellent. To which I had grown immune. But I avoided breathing deeply, conscious of germs. The next cubicle was cleaner. Sodden toilet paper on the floor and an old newspaper scrunched up behind the bowl. The floor was littered with the evidence of sex that had taken place earlier. Perhaps only minutes earlier: you could smell it. The water in the bowl was brown. I pushed the button and the toilet rushed into a violent flush. Good. The hard metal rim was mottled with dried filth and I disconnected myself from my legs as I sat down on it. *You filthy deranged cunt. You pervert. How low can you go? Is this it? Sitting in shit you can no longer even smell. If they could see you now. You poor bastard.*

There was no-one. I was alone, sitting shotgun, alert to the tiniest noise, as tight as a wire. Poised on the toilet like a dog about to take a shit, my back slightly rounded, my legs bent and tense, ready to spring up and fight for my life if it was required. The door lock was half-turned in accordance with an unspoken international language of sexual invitation. The wind outside punched the iron roof, colluding with my nerves and the violent stories I'd heard about bashings and rapes, but I held my ground and waited. A car braked in the car park behind me, people walked past outside, a door slammed in the distance, and a dog barked, then nothing. The back of the cubicle door was spattered with the dried fluids of other men. The smell from the cubicle next door defined itself more sharply the longer I waited. It pinched inside my nose, registering my level of commitment and depravity. Outside a car alarm bleeped and all the locks crashed down at once, safe and secure. The gravel outside the door crunched. Someone entered. Someone walked to the urinal. Unzipped, urinated, flushed. I tightened up. Someone walked over to the sink and turned on the water. The water off and I heard nothing. I started to let out a long, quiet breath. Blood rushed at the vessels of my face and I blushed like an idiot. Someone didn't move. Time and space convulsed to suspend me between the people I might become. *I'm taking a shit until you show me otherwise. I'm no fag. See I'm using toilet paper. I'm legit. Breathe. Take in air. Not too deep, the germs remember, the smell. Come on man, what are you doing? Move. Move. Give me a sign. Push on the door. Come closer. Show me who I am.* Terror had me, but I'd learned to dull it. I wiped away fear with resignation and waited.

WARNING

Due to increased
criminal activity these
premises are now under
24HR continuous
Police patrol.

Acknowledgments

Thank you to the many people who encouraged and supported me to write this novel, especially Marion Campbell, Kenton Miller, Jacqui Cussen, Joan Nestle and Frank Bonnici. Parts of this work first appeared in *Traffic* and *Strange Shapes*.

www.ingramcontent.com/pod-product-compliance
Lightning Source LLC
Chambersburg PA
CBHW071251250626
47163CB00002B/424